Vox

Nicholson Baker was born in 1957. He has written three other novels, *Room Temperature*, *The Mezzanine* and *The Fermata*. He is also the author of a non-fiction book, *U and I*, and a book of essays, *The Size of Thoughts*. He lives in California.

NICHOLSON BAKER

Vox

Granta Books

London

Granta Publications, 2/3 Hanover Yard, London N1 8BE

First published in the USA by Random House Inc. 1992
First published in Great Britain by Granta Books 1992
This edition published by Granta Books 1998

A CIP catalogue record for this book is available
from the British Library.

3 5 7 9 10 8 6 4 2

Printed and bound in Great Britain
by Mackays of Chatham PLC

"What are you wearing?" he asked.

She said, "I'm wearing a white shirt with little stars, green and black stars, on it, and black pants, and socks the color of the green stars, and a pair of black sneakers I got for nine dollars."

"What are you doing?"

"I'm lying on my bed, which is made. That's an unusual thing. I made my bed this morning. A few months ago my mother gave me a chenille bedspread, exactly the kind we used to have, and I felt bad that it was still folded up unused and this morning I finally made the bed with it."

"I don't know what chenille is," he said. "It's some kind of silky material?"

"No, it's cotton. Cotton chenille. It's got those little tufts, in conventional patterns. Like in bed-and-breakfasts."

"Oh oh oh, the patterns of *tufts*. I'm relieved."

"Why?" she asked.

"Silk is somehow . . . you think of ads for escort services where the type is set in fake-o eighteenth-century script—*For the Discriminating Gentleman*—that kind of thing. Or Deliques Intimates, you know that catalog?"

"I get one about every week."

7

"Right, a deluge. Lace filigree, Aubrey Beardsley, no thank you. All I can think of is, ma'am, those silk tap pants you've got on are going to stain."

"You're right about that," she said. "Someone gave me this exotic chemisey thing, not from Deliques but the same idea, silk with lace. I get quite . . . I get very *moist* when I'm aroused, it's almost embarrassing actually. So this chemisey thing got soaked. He said, the person who bought it for me said, 'So what, throw it away, use it once.' But I don't know, I thought I might want to wear it again. It's really nice to wear silk, you know. So I took it to the dry cleaners. I didn't mention it specifically, I bunched it in with a lot of work clothes. It came back with a little tag on it, with a little dancing man with a tragic expression, wearing a hat, who says, you know, 'Sorry! We did everything we could, we took extraordinary measures, but the stains on this garment could not come out!' I took a look at it, and it was very odd, there were these five *dot* stains on it, little ovals, not down where I'd been wet, but higher up, on the front."

"Weird."

"And the guy who gave it to me had *not* come on me. He came elsewhere—that much I was sure of. So my theory is that someone at the dry cleaners . . ."

"No! Do you still give them your business?"

"Well, they're convenient."

"Where do you live?"

"In an eastern city."

"Oh. I live in a western city."

"How nice."

"It is nice," he said. "From my window I can see a streetlight with lots of spike holes in it, from utility workers—I mean a wooden telephone pole with a streetlight on it—"

"Of course."

"And a few houses. The streetlight is photo-activated, and watching it come on is really one of the most beautiful things."

"What time is it there?"

"Um—six-twelve," he said.

"Is it dark there yet?"

"No. Is it there?"

"Not completely," she said. "It doesn't feel really dark to me until the little lights on my stereo receiver are the brightest things in the room. That's not strictly true, but it sounds good, don't you think? What hand are you holding the phone with?"

"My left," he said.

"What are you doing with your right hand?"

"My right hand is, at the moment, my fingers are resting in the soil of a potted plant somebody gave me, that isn't doing too well. I'm sort of moving my fingers in the soil."

"What kind of a plant?"

"I can't remember," he said. "The soil has several round polished stones stuck in it. Oh wait, here's the tag.

No, that's just the price tag. An anonymous mystery plant."

"You haven't told me what *you're* wearing," she said.

"I am wearing . . . I'm wearing, well, a bathrobe, and flip-flops with blue soles and red holder-onners. I'm new to flip-flops—I mean since moving out here. They're good in the morning for waking up. On weekends I put them on and I walk down to the corner and buy the paper, and the feeling of that thong right in the crotch of your toe—man, it pulls you together, it starts your day. It's like putting your feet in a bridle."

"Are you 'into' feet?" she asked.

"No no no no no no no no. On women? No. They're neutral. They're about like elbows. In my *own* case, I do . . ."

"What?"

"Well, I do very often, when I'm about to come, I seem to like to rise up on the balls of my feet. It's something about the tension of all the leg muscles and the, you know, the ass muscles, it puts all the nerves in communication, it's as if I'm coming with my legs. On the other hand, when I do it I sometimes feel like some kind of high school teacher, bouncing on his heels, or like some kind of demagogue, rising up on tiptoe and roaring out something about destiny."

"And then, at the very top of your *relevé*, you come into a tissue," she said.

"Yep."

"The things we do for love. I knew this person, a doctor, who once told me that he liked to hyperventilate when he was masturbating, like a puppy. He got very scientific about it. He said that hyperventilating decreases the ionized calcium in the blood, alters neural conductivity, does this, does that. I tried it once. He said when you're almost there, after panting and panting, he-a-he-a-he-a, you're supposed to do this thing called a Valsalva, which is where you take a breath and you clamp your throat shut and push *hard*, and if you do it right, you're supposed to have a mind-blowing orgasm—tingling extremities, tingling roots of your hair, tingling teeth, I don't know, the whole business. I didn't have much success with the technique, but he was this huge man, huge coarse beard, huge arms, he loved large meatball subs, with that orange grease—and he was so big and so innocent and actually quite shy that the idea of him gasping—"

"His eyes squinted shut."

"Right, hunched over his male organ, though I have to say I was never quite able to picture his male organ, but the idea of him intentionally, deliberately gasping and swallowing was enough to help me toward a moment or two of pleasure myself."

"Ooo. On that very bed?"

"On this very bed."

"But without the chenille bedspread."

"Without the chenille bedspread, which I notice is

11

leaving little white pieces of fluff on my pants, mm, mm, mm, get off, you. You see, a pretentiously sexy silk bedspread from Deliques would have been more practical after all."

"Well, right, no, I can see that the things in Deliques might be sexy," he said. "Garters and all that. They don't do much for me—in fact, the whole Victorian flavor of a certain kind of smirky kinkiness puts me off—but still, I have to admit that when the catalogs started coming, week after week, early fall, midfall, late fall, this persistent gush of half-dressed women flowing toward me in the mail, on such expensive paper, with the bee-stung lips and all that, it did start to interest me."

"Ah, now you're admitting it," she said. "The male models are quite good-looking, too."

"Well, but still for me it wasn't the lace hemi-demi-camisoles or any of that. I'll tell you what it was, in fact. It was this one picture of a woman wearing a loose green shirt, lying on her back, with her legs in the air, crossed at the ankles, wearing a pair of tights. Not black tights. I was, I was absolutely entranced by this picture. I remember coming home from work and sitting at the kitchen table, studying this picture for about . . . ten minutes, reading the little description of the tights, looking at the picture again, reading, looking. She had very long legs. Now, did I have anybody I could buy these tights for? No, not really. Not at that moment. They were made of a certain kind of stitch, not chenille, not chenille. Pointelle! She was wearing these beigey-green pointelle tights. See, to me the word 'tights' is much more exciting than just 'stockings.' Anyway I went into the living room and put the phone on the floor, and then I lay down on the floor next to the phone and I just studied this shot, went through the rest of the catalog, but back to this one picture again, until my arms started to get tired from holding the pages in the air, and I put the catalog face-down on my chest, and I went into a state of pure bliss, rolling my head back and forth on the rug. If you roll your head back and forth on the floor it usually increases any feeling of awe or wonder that you've got going. But no tingling of the extremities, unfortunately."

"No."

"And I don't eat lots of meatball subs. I mean I *do* enjoy a meatball sub occasionally, with mushrooms—I just want to differentiate myself from, you know . . ."

"Oh don't worry about that," she said. "Your accent is very different from his, your voice is quite . . . compelling."

"I'm glad to hear that. I was nervous when I called. My temperature dropped about fifteen degrees as I was deciding to dial the number."

"Really. Where did you see the ad?"

"Ah, a men's magazine."

"Which one?" she asked.

"This is oddly embarrassing. *Juggs*. *Juggs* magazine. Where did you see the ad?"

There was a pause. *"Forum."*

"What does your ad say?" he asked.

"Let me see," she said. "There's a line drawing of a man and a woman, each holding a telephone, and the headline is ANYTIME AT ALL. I liked the drawing."

"I've seen that one," he said. "That's very different from my ad. My ad has a color shot of a woman with a phone cord wrapped around her leg and one arm kind of covering her breasts, and the headline over the phone number is, MAKE IT HAPPEN. But there *is* something intangibly classier about this ad than the other ads, something about the layout and the type that the phone number is in, despite the usual woman-plus-phone image, and I thought that maybe it might attract a different sort of caller. Although, boy, that flurry of assholic horniness from the men on the line when you first spoke was not exactly cucumber sandwich conversation. That *one* guy that kept interrupting—'You like to *sock* on a big *caulk?*' 'How big and brown are your nips?' But then, I suppose we aren't calling for cucumber sandwich conversation."

"I wouldn't object—cucumber away. But I guess not. Anyhow, here we are, 'one on one,' as they say, in the famous fiber-optical 'back room.' "

"True enough."

"So go on," she said. "You were telling me how you were on the floor rolling your head back and forth?"

"Oh, right. Well, I was on the floor with the catalog

facedown on my chest, entranced by those tights, and a conception, this conception of thrilling wrongness, took shape in my brain stem. I had a vision of myself jerking off while I ordered that pair of tights, specifically the vision was of, of, of . . ."

"Of?"

"Of being in the bathtub, but on the phone with the order-taker from Deliques, who's got, you know, this nice innocent voice, a mistaken but lovable overfrizzed perm, a hint of twang, bland face, freshly laundered jeans, cute socks, but probably wearing a pair of Deliques finest 'fusion panties' with a chevron of lace or something over her mound, which she's bought at the employee discount, while I'm in my bathtub, which is ridiculous since I never take baths, but I'm in my bathtub moving so carefully so she won't hear any aquatic splips or splaps and know that I've taken the portable phone into the bathroom and that I'm semi-submerged, and she says, 'Let me check to be sure we have that in stock for you, sir,' and during the pause, I arch myself up out of the water and sort of point the phone at my Werner Heisenberg so she can see it somehow or get its vibes, and at the moment she says, 'Yes, we do have the pointelle tights in faun,' I come, in perfect silence, making a Smurf grimace."

"That's awful."

"I know, but I don't know, I was there on the living-room floor. I don't often lie down there."

"Were you actually . . . playing with yourself as you envisioned this?"

"Certainly not! I had one hand on the telephone, just *toying* with the number keys, teasing them, and the other hand was lying on the facedown catalog on my chest. Anyway, then I thought I would be embarrassed to order a pair of tights for myself—maybe the order-taker would assume that I was a transsexual, when in fact I am not a transsexual at all, I'm a telephone clitician."

"An obscene phone caller."

"Exactly. And I started to think of who I could order them for, and I thought of this woman at work, a very nice woman, some might say plain, but very nice, who once startled me and this other guy by telling a story out of the blue about some friends of hers who'd just had a large wedding at a museum during which some thieves backed a van up and loaded all the wedding gifts in and drove away."

"The wedding gifts were on display?" she asked.

"Yes."

"Ah, well, that was their mistake."

"Well, they were punished for it. Anyway, one of the gifts, this woman from work told us, was one of those sex slings that I guess you bolt to a stud in the ceiling, so that the woman is . . ."

"Yeah, I know," she said.

"And this woman from work had joked about the difficulty of trying to fence the stolen sex sling, and the memory of her talking about this oddball device came back to me and I wanted to order the tights for her, so she'd come home from work one day, and she'd go, 'Hey, what's this, a slim little package for me from De-liques?' She'd open it up and slip out this plastic packet with tights in it, and there's the order slip in her hand, and somehow I've convinced the order-taker that I don't want my name on the slip."

"Sure, sure."

"So she knows she's got a secret admirer. And there on the packing slip is the line of printout that says, all in abbreviations, 1 PR PTL TIGHTS, FN, SM, $12.95, and I just thought of her looking at the packing slip and think-ing, Well, gee, I suppose I *should* at least see if they fit."

"Ah, but wait," she said. "No, what catches her eye, what catches her eye is . . ."

"Tell me," he said.

"Is that on the packing slip, over the numeral one, for one pair of tights, is this *check mark*, in blunt pencil."

"That's right, there is."

"And she looks closely at that check mark, and she imagines a male hand making it, a surprisingly refined hand, because there has been a strike at the Deliques warehouse, and what's happened is that Deliques man-agement has had to hire the male models from the cat-alog on an emergency basis to fill in for the normal pickers and packers, who are of course mostly middle-aged Laotian women. And they were right in the middle

of a catalog shoot, all these male models, when the walk-out took place, so they're wearing exactly what they were wearing on the shoot, which are the usual aubergine paisley boxer shorts, and Henri Rousseau bathrobes, and Erté pajamas, and that sort of thing, but there was no time for them to change, they had to be herded barefoot into this giant warehouse because the company was bombed with orders. April was their biggest month. So—one male model takes this woman's order slip, and studies it, looks at her name on it—what's her name?"

"Jill."

"Looks at her name, Jill Smith, and then takes the order slip and crumples it against the piece of horseradish in his foulard silk boxer shorts, and he hands it to the next male model, a gorgeous peasant with strange slitty nipples, who smooths it out, studies it, duh, Jill Smith, squeezes his asscheeks together, and passes it to the next guy, who smooths it out, studies it, bites one corner, and hands it to the next guy, and so on down this row of male models, each one broader-shouldered and sinewier-stomached than the last, until finally the order slip gets to the last guy, who's fallen asleep sitting on one tang of the forklift, a much slighter gentleman, with a beautiful throat with a softly pulsing jugular you just wanted to *eat* it looked so good, and of course wearing a green moiré silk codpiece, pushed forward and upward by the one tang of the forklift. This male model rouses himself, smacks his lips sleepily, studies the slip of paper, gets in the forklift, and drives off, weaves off, toward the distant vault where they keep the pointelle tights."

"Yes?"

"And he reaches the mountain of crates marked FAUN, and he slides the forklift into the highest pallet and lifts it off and, *vvvvvvvv*, brings it down, and he pries it open . . ."

"Probably with his dick."

"No, no, with his powerful refined *hands*," she said. "The packing tape goes *pap! pap! pap!* as he tears the mighty box asunder. But now that you mention it, as he's reaching in, deep into the box filled with . . . with one metric ton of cotton pointelle, his cock *is* pressing against the cardboard, pressing, pressing, and it starts to fight against the tethers of that codpiece. So he climbs back in the forklift, puts the pair of tights in his lap, and drives back. Well, while he was gone, Todd, Rod, Sod, and Wadd, the other male models, all heterosexual, of course, who've been standing in a row waiting for him, have been thinking about Jill Smith wearing those tights and by now their bobolinks have all gotten thoroughly hard, and even the sleepy forklift driver, perhaps because of the faun tights in his lap, is embarrassed to get out because there's this frank erection that has now gotten so big and bone-hard that it's angling right out of his codpiece. He takes his place in the row of male models, his cock swaying slightly, and he holds the tights to his face and exhales through them, then nods, takes a pencil with a surprisingly sharp point, and makes a check mark over the numeral one on the packing slip. He hands it to the next guy—by this time all the male models have abandoned their shame in each other's presence and they are all standing there in a row with their various organs pronging at various angles out of their various robes and boxers and sex-briefs. So the forklift guy hands it to the next guy, who almost ritualistically takes the tights and winds them around and around his cock, pulls once hard, and then unwinds them and makes a check mark exactly superimposed over the first check mark on the numeral one on the packing slip. And he hands the tights to the next guy, who also winds the tights around his cock, many winds, it's *very* long, and he pulls, and he makes a superimposing check mark, too, and so on down the row, wind unwind check, wind unwind check, and the final guy folds the tights up with neat agile movements that belie his enormous forearms and slides them into the sheer plastic envelope and puts the last check mark over the numeral one, so that it now looks as if only one blunt pencil check-marked over it, when really there were *nine* check marks. And so together, humming 'The Volga Boatman' in unison, they seal the package up with Jill Smith's address on it and send it off to her."

"Well, maybe that *is* what happened," he said. "No, in reality, there wasn't any strike at Deliques when I called. Their computer was down, though."

"Oh, so you really *did* call?" she said. "That's very wicked of you. In the bath?"

"No, in the end that seemed like too much trouble. I called from the living-room floor. First I worked myself up to a creditable state of engorgement, then I dialed the 800 number."

"All right . . ."

"A woman answered and said something like 'Hello and welcome to Deliques Intimates, this is Clititia speaking, how may we help you today?' She had a young high voice, exactly the sort of voice I'd imagined. Well, my fourteen-and-a-half-inch sperm-dowel instantly shrank to less than three inches. Which is the opposite of what was supposed to happen. I told her what I wanted to order, and she said the computer was down, but she would take the order 'by hand,' right? Why wasn't I enough of a leerer to come back with something insinuating? Just something basic, like 'Heh heh, honey, I hope you *do* take it all by hand.' But instead I just said, 'Boy oh boy, that must be a lot of trouble for you.' I gave her my address, my card number, and she said, 'I've got that, sir, now, is there anything else you would like to order this evening?' I said, 'Well, I'm torn, there *is* one other thing I'd like to get this person, just a pair of very simple panties, but I'm torn.' I said, 'Now you see the so-called Deliques *minimes* on page thirty-eight? You see those? Do you have the catalog there right in front of you?' She said she did. I said, 'Okay. I'm not sure I can tell the difference between these *minimes* and the so-called *nadja pants* on page, ah, forty-six. To the naked eye they seem identical.' She said, 'Just one moment,' and I heard her flipping through the catalog, and I made a last valiant attempt to stroke myself off, because the idea of her looking carefully at those pictures of women in those tiny weightless panties, with the darkness of pubic hair visible right *there* through the material, at the very same time I was looking at those same cuppable curves of pubic hair on my end, should have been enough to make me shoot instantly, but I don't know, she sounded so well-meaning, and I knew that there was a very good chance that she would not like to know that I was there trying to . . . I mean, she didn't want to work at a job where men called her and ordered a few items of merchandise just so they could . . . right? That wasn't what she'd had in mind at all in taking the job, or possibly wasn't, at least, so even when she said, finally, 'Well, the nadja pants ride a little lower on the hip,' which is a statement that any normal jacker-offer should be able to come to easily, because what does it imply? It implies her own hip, it implies that the nadja panties have ridden *her own hip*. But even then I could not achieve and maintain. So I said, 'Oh well, no, thanks, I'll see how the tights go over and then order the *minimes* later.' And a week afterward, I was the owner of a pair of tights. I still have them, unopened. Give me your address and I'll be glad to forward them to you."

"Why don't you give them to Jill?" she asked.

"Oh, a million reasons. But that's not quite the end. I hung up from making the order and instantly I got hard again, naturally, and I thought for a second, and I hit the redial button, and a different woman answered, with a much lower and smarter voice, with some name like Vulva, and I said, 'Vulva, I have what may sound like an unorthodox question, and you don't have to answer it if you don't want to. But what I'm curious about is, well, of the men who order from your catalog, do you think some of them are in a subtle or maybe not-so-subtle way obscene phone callers?' She laughed and she said, 'That's a good question.' And then there was a long pause, a very long pause. I said, 'Hello?' And right there I knew I'd blown it—I knew the tone of my hello, that slight reediness in my voice that betrayed sexual tension, blew away the potential rapport I might have had with Vulva. See, I'd sounded quite confident when I actually asked her the question."

"What did she say?"

"She just said, in a more official voice, but still a friendly voice, 'I don't think I'm going to answer your question.' And I said, 'Fine, I understand, okay, sure.' And she said 'Bye.' Not 'Good-bye,' you notice—still the slight vestige of amused intimacy there. If she'd said 'Good-bye' I would have felt absolutely crushed."

"What did you do then?"

"I sat up and ordered a pizza and read the paper. So you see, I'm not an obscene phone caller, really. I can't smother an orgasm."

"Ho ho. I can," she said.

23

"Can you? Well, I mean I can physically do it."

"*I* know what you mean."

There was a pause.

"I hear ice cubes," he said.

"Diet Coke."

"Ah. Tell me more things. Tell me about the room you're in. Tell me the chain of events that led up to your calling this number."

"Okay," she said. "I'm not in the bedroom anymore. I'm sitting on the couch in my living room slash dining room. My feet are on the coffee table, which would have been impossible yesterday, because the coffee table was piled so high with mail and work stuff, but now it is possible, and the whole room, the whole apartment, is really and truly in order. I took a sick day today, without being sick, which is something I haven't done up to now at this job. I called the receptionist and told her I had a fever. The moment of lying to her was awful, but gosh what freedom when I hung up the phone! And I didn't leave the apartment all day. I just organized my immediate surroundings, I picked up things, I vacuumed, and I laid out all the silver that I've inherited—three different very incomplete patterns—laid it out on the dining-room table and looked at it and I gave some serious thought to polishing it, but I didn't go so far as to polish it, but it looked beautiful all laid out, a big arch of forks, a little arch of knives, five big serving spoons, some tiny salt spoons, and a little grouping of novelty items, like oyster forks. No teaspoons at all. One of the dinner forks from my great aunt's set fell into the dishwasher once when I was visiting her and it got badly notched by that twirly splasher in the bottom, and someone at work was telling me he knew a jeweler who fixed hurt silverware, so I'm planning to have that fixed, it's all ready to go. And I even got together all my broken sets of beads—I sorted them all out—the sight of all those beads jumbled together on my bedside table was making me unhappy every morning, and now they're ready to be restrung, the pink ones in one envelope, and the green ones in one envelope, and the parti-colored Venetian ones in one envelope—and I have them on my dining-room table too, ready to go."

"The same jeweler who fixes silverware restrings beads?" he asked.

"Yes!"

"How did your beads get broken?"

"They seem to break in the morning when I'm rushing to get dressed. They catch on something. The jade ones, my favorite set, which my father gave me, caught on the open door of the microwave when I was standing up too quickly after picking a piece of paper up off the floor. That was the latest tragedy. And of course my sister's babe yanked one set off my neck. But they can all be repaired and they will all be repaired."

"Good going."

"Anyway, this apartment is transformed, I mean it,

not just superficially but with new hidden pockets of order in it, and I waited until the midafternoon to have a shower, and I did *not* masturbate, because the illicitness of calling in sick without justification made me want to be pure and virtuous all day long, and I had an early dinner of Carr's Table Water crackers with cream cheese and sliced pieces of sweet red kosher peppers on them, just delicious, and I did *not* turn on the TV but instead I turned on the stereo, which I haven't used much lately. It's a very fancy stereo."

"Yes?"

"I think I spent something like fourteen hundred dollars on it," she said. "I bought it from someone who was buying an even fancier system. It was true insanity. I had a crush on this person. He liked the Thompson Twins and the S.O.S. Band and, gee, what were the other groups he liked so much? The Gap Band was one. Midnight Star. And Cameo. This was a while ago. He was not a particularly intelligent man, in fact in a way he was a very dimwitted narrow-minded man, but he was *so* infectiously convinced that what he liked everyone would like if they were exposed to it. And good-looking. For about four months, while I was in his thrall, I really *listened* to that stuff. I gave my life up to it. My own taste in music stopped evolving in grade school with the Beatles, the early early Beatles—in fact I used to dislike any song that didn't end—you know, end with a chord, but simply faded out."

"But then you met this guy," he said.

"Exactly!" she said. "All of the songs he liked faded out, or most of them did. And so I became a connoisseur of fade-outs. I bought cassettes. I used to turn them up very loud—with the headphones on—and listen very closely, trying to catch that precise moment when the person in the recording studio had begun to turn my volume dial down, or whatever it was he did. Sometimes I'd turn the volume dial up at just the speed I thought he—I mean the ghostly hand of the record producer— was turning it down, so that the sound stayed on an even plane. I'd get in this sort of trance, like you on the rug, where I thought if I kept turning it up—and this is a very powerful amplifier, mind you—the song would not stop, it would just continue indefinitely. And so what I had thought of before as just a kind of artistic sloppiness, this attempt to imply that oh yeah, we're a bunch of endlessly creative folks who jam all night, and the bad old record producer finally has to turn down the volume on us just so we don't fill the whole album with one monster song, became for me instead this kind of, this kind of summation of hopefulness. I first felt it in a song called 'Ain't Nobody,' which was a song that this man I had the crush on was particularly keen on. 'Ain't nobody, loves me better.' You know that one?"

"You sing well!" he said.

"I do not. But that's the song, and as you get toward the end of it, a change takes place in the way you hear it,

27

which is that the knowledge that the song is going to end starts to be more important than the specific ups and downs of the melody, and even though the singer is singing just as loud as ever, in fact she's really pouring it on now, she's fighting to be heard, it's as if you are hearing the inevitable waning of popularity of that hit, its slippage down the charts, and the twilight of the career of the singer, despite all of the beautiful subtle things she's able to do with a plain old dumb old bunch of notes, and even as she goes for one last high note, full of daring and hope and passionateness and everything worthwhile, she's lost, she's sinking down."

"Oh! Don't *cry!*" he said. "I'm not equipped . . . I mean my comforting skills don't have that kind of range."

There was another sound of ice cubes. She said, "It's just that I really liked him. Vain bum. We went dancing one night, and I made the mistake of suggesting to him as we were on the dance floor that maybe he should take his pen out of his shirt pocket and put it in his back pocket. And that was it, he never called me again."

"That little scum-twirler! Tell me his address, I'll fade *him* out, I'll rip his arms off."

"No. I got over it. Anyway, that wasn't what I meant to talk about. I just mean I was here in my wonderfully orderly apartment after dinner and I saw this big joke of a stereo system and I switched it on, and the sky got darker and all the little red and green lights on the receiver were like ocean buoys or something, and I started to feel what you'd expect, sad, happy, resigned, horny, some combination of all of them, and I felt suddenly that I'd been virtuous for long enough and probably should definitely masturbate, and I thought wait, let's not just have a perfunctory masturbation session, Abby, let's do something just a little bit special tonight, to round out a special day, right? So I brought out a copy of *Forum* that I rather bravely bought one day a while ago. But I'd read all the stories and all the letters and it just wasn't working. So I started looking at the ads, really almost for the first time. And there was this headline: ANYTIME AT ALL."

"MAKE IT HAPPEN."

"That's right. And I *like* the sound of the pauses in long-distance conversations—the cassette hiss sound. And yet I didn't really want to talk to anyone I knew. So that's more or less why I called. Now I've answered your questions, now you tell me something."

"Do you want to hear something true, or something imaginary?"

"First true, then imaginary," she said.

"Once," he said, "I was listening to the stereo with the headphones on, I was about sixteen, and the stereo receiver was on the floor of a little room off the living room, I don't know why it was on the floor, I guess because my father was repainting the living room—that must have been it—and the headphone cord was quite short, but I was very interested in learning how to dance. It was winter, it was maybe eight o'clock at night, very

29

dark, I hadn't turned on the light in the room. And I was trying to learn all these moves, but tethered to the stereo, so I was almost completely doubled over, like I was tracking some animal, but I was really ecstatic—dancing, sweating, out of breath, flailing my arms, doing little jumps . . . once I got a little too excited and did a *big* sideways bob of my head and the headphones came off and pulled my glasses off with them—but no problem, I just stylized the motions of picking up my glasses and putting them on and repeated them a few times, incorporated them in. And then suddenly I hear, 'Jim, *what* are you doing?' in this horrified voice. My younger sister had heard all this breathing and panting coming from me in the darkness and thought of course that I was . . ."

"Right."

"I said, 'I'm dancing.' And she went away. I danced for a while longer, but with somewhat less conviction. That was my year of heavy stereo use. Unlike you I didn't have a big crush on anyone at the time. I think it was more that I had a crush on the tuner itself, frankly. I used to imagine that the megahertz markings were the skyline of a city at night. The FM markings were all the buildings, and the AM markings were their reflection in water . . ."

"Ah," she said, "but you're supposed to be telling me something true, not something imagined."

"Yes, but the true thing is shading into the imagined thing, all right? And the little moving indicator on our stereo was lit with a yellow light, and I knew where all the stations were on the dial, and I'd spin the knob and the yellow indicator would glide up and down the radio cityscape like a cab up and down some big central boulevard, and each station was an intersection, in a neighborhood with a different ethnic mix, and if the red sign came on saying STEREO I might idle there for a while, or the cabbie might run the light, passing the whole thing by as it exploded and disappeared behind me. And sometimes I'd thumb the dial very slowly, sort of like I was palming a steering wheel, and move up, move up, in the silence of the muted stretches, and then suddenly I'd pierce the rind of a station and there would be this crackling hopped-up luridly colored version of a song that sounded for a second much better than I knew the song really was, like that moment in solar eclipses when the whole corona is visible, and then you slide down into the fertile valley of the station itself, and it spreads out beneath you, in stereo, with a whole range of middle and misty distances."

"That's true!" she said.

"It *is* true? That's bad, because it means that I still have to come up with an imaginary thing, right?"

"I'm afraid so."

"But my imagination doesn't work that way," he said. "It doesn't just hop to at the snap of a finger. What do you want the imaginary thing I tell you to be about?"

"I think that it should be about . . . my beads and my silverware, since they're all laid out for us."

"Well," he said. There was a pause. "Once there was

a guy who, um, needed his fork repaired. No, I can't. I'm sorry. You tell me something more."

"It's *your* turn."

"I need more confidences from you first. I need to be charged up with a stream of confidences flowing from you to me."

"Come on now," she said. "Give it a try."

"Yeah, but I don't think I can just be handed an assignment like that. I'm pedestrian. I think I have to stay with the truth."

"All right, tell me what the most recent thing or event was that aroused you."

"The idea of making this call," he said.

"Before that."

"Let me think back," he said. "The Walt Disney character of Tinker Bell. I was just leaving the video store, and I came to this big cardboard display of *Peter Pan*, the Walt Disney cartoon *Peter Pan*, which has just been rereleased, with a TV beside it playing the movie."

"When was this?"

"This was today, about an hour and a half ago, I guess. I rented three X-rated tapes."

"And you're going to play them later this evening?"

"Maybe. Maybe not, I don't know. I was going to play them when I got home."

"The second you got home."

"That's right."

"What about dinner?"

"I ate at a pizza place."

"What kind?"

"Small mushroom anchovy."

"All right. So you got home with the tapes . . ."

"Yeah, and I put them on top of the TV and got out of my work clothes and put on a bathrobe . . ."

"Just a bathrobe?"

"Well, I have my T-shirt and underwear on underneath, of course."

"White underwear?"

"Gray, white, somewhere in that range. Anyway, I came out and saw the pile of X-rated tapes on top of my TV, and they're in these orange boxes. The store uses brown boxes for their normal tapes, like adventure, comedy, slasher, etcetera, and then they use a whole different color, an orange box, for the adult tapes. It's to avoid confusion, because now there are so many X-rated Christmas tapes and X-rated versions of *Cinderella* and all that. And I'd never seen two of these particular tapes before, but of course I knew what was in them anyway, and I heartily approved of it, I'm enthusiastically pro-pornography, obviously, but suddenly I foresaw my own crude arousal—I saw myself fast-forwarding through the numbing parts, trying to find some image that was good, or at least good enough to come to, and the sound of the VCR as it fast-forwards, that industrial robot sound, and I suddenly thought no, no, even though one of the tapes has got Lisa Melendez in it, who I think is just . . .

delightful, I thought no, I don't want to see these right now. Fortunately, I'd also bought a *Juggs* magazine, because this anti-orange-tape reaction has hit me before. There are just times when you want a fixed image."

"There's always the pause button," she suggested.

"Well, but then you get those white sawtooth lines across the screen."

"Four heads are better than two, as they say. Of course, the resolution is better on the magazine page, I imagine."

"It certainly is," he said. "But it's much more than that! Don't laugh, really. No movie still is ever as good as a photograph. A photograph catches a woman at a point where her frans are at their perfect point of expressiveness—the soul of her frans is revealed, or rather the souls *are* revealed, because each has a separate personality. Nipples in still pictures are as varied and as communicative as women's eyes, or almost."

"Frans?"

"Yeah, sometimes I don't like the word 'breasts' and all those slangish synonyms. I mean, just look at the drop in arousingness between *Playboy* magazine and the exact same women when they're *moving* from pose to pose on the *Playboy* channel. It's true that I don't actually get the *Playboy* channel, so I see everything on it through those houndstooth and herringbone cycles of the scrambling circuit, and I keep flipping back and forth between it and the two channels on either side of it because sometimes for an instant the picture is startled into visibility just after you switch the channel, and you'll catch this bright yellow torso and one full fran with a fire-engine-red nipple, and then it teeters, it falters, and collapses—and I've noticed that the scrambling works least well and you can see things best when nothing is moving in the TV image, i.e., when it's a TV image *of* a magazine image, sort of as if the scrambling circuitry is overcome in the same way I am sometimes overcome by the power of fixed pictures. I once stayed up until two-thirty in the morning doing this, flipping."

"Anyway."

"Right. Anyway, I looked through my brand-new *Juggs* magazine with high hopes, but I don't know—again, the sexiest woman was in a poolside setting, and I find poolside settings unerotic—that is to say, in general I find them unerotic, since God knows I've certainly come to an enormous number of poolside layouts in magazines, but there's something about the publicness of its being outside, in the sun—it's not as bad as a beach setting, which is a complete turnoff—I mean, again, if I were exiled to a desert island with nothing but some pages of a men's magazine showing a nude woman on a desert island, with the arty kidney shapes of sand on the ass-cheeks and all that, I would probably break down and masturbate to it . . . what do you think of that word?"

" 'Masturbate'? I don't hate it. I don't love it."

"Let's get a new word for it," he said.

"To myself, I sometimes call it 'dithering myself off.' "

"Okay, a possibility. What about just 'fiddle'? Fiddlin' yourself off? The dropped *g* is kind of racy. No, no. *Strum*."

"Strum."

"That's it. I looked through the *Juggs*, and even though it was a poolside scene, I tried to *strum*, and there *was* one shot where the woman was looking straight at me, on her elbows on a yellow pool raft, and her frans were at their point of perfect beauty, not erect nipples but soft rounded tolerant nipples, which you have to have in a poolside photo set because as soon as you see those erect nipples in a poolside layout you think *cold water*, you don't think arousal. I want you to know, by the way, that I am not one of these sad individuals who hang out at the frozen fried-chicken section of the supermarket where it's extra cold just to see women's nipples get hard. I don't get the least thrill from wet T-shirt contests either, because I have to have an answering arousal there in the woman, and cold water is anti-sexual, except if in the case of the wet T-shirt contest I can convince myself that this woman is using the shock of the cold water, the giggliness and the splutteriness of it, to make something possible that otherwise wouldn't be possible and yet is arousing to her: I mean if she *wants* to show off her breasts, if she's proud of them and yet knows she's not the kind of person who's going to go off and become a stripper or whatever, and the douse of cold water is distracting enough to keep her sense of its all being in innocent fun in the end, *then* I can get turned on by shots of a wet T-shirt contest. You know?"

"I can see how that works. So you're looking at the woman in *Juggs*."

"Yes, and she was looking right at me, so appealingly, with such a lucid joyful amused look and her elbows were really digging into the pillow of the yellow raft, so it looked as if it might burst, and I could almost imagine strumming myself off to this, but then, no, there were too many things wrong—the photographer had put her hair in pigtails, tied with some kind of thick purply pink polyester yarn, and it just seemed so awful somehow, the age-old thing of men wanting to pretend that twenty-eight-year-old women are little girls by forcing this icon of girlishness, pigtails, on them, when really, when was the last time you saw a real little girl wearing pigtails? Not to *mention* the incidental fact that little girls are a turnoff. Here's this beautiful, alert, lovely woman, of at least twenty-seven, and all I could see was the dickhead photographer handing her some polyester yarn and saying, 'Uhright, now tie this purple stuff in your hair.' And I felt at that moment that I wanted to talk to a real woman, no more images of any kind, no fast forward, no pause, no magazine pictures. And there was the ad."

"But you've called these numbers before, haven't you?" she asked.

"A few times, but with no real success. And I don't

think I've ever called this very number before—2VOX."

"What do you mean by 'success'?"

"No women with any kind of spark. Or, actually, honestly, few women at all, period, except the ones who are paid by the phone service to make mechanical sexual small talk and moan occasionally. It's mostly just men saying 'Hey, any ladies out there?' But then once in a while a real woman will call. And at least with this, as opposed to pictures, at least there's the remote possibility of something clicking. Perhaps it's presumptuous of me to say that we, you and I, click, but there is that possibility."

"Yes."

"In a way it's like the radio. Do you know that I've never actually gone to a store and bought a record? That's probably why I never learned to appreciate the fade-out, as you describe it, since on the radio, one song melts into the next. But it seems to me that you really need the feeling of radio luck in listening to pop music, since after all it's about somebody meeting, out of all the zillions of people in the world, this one other nice person, or at least several adequate people. And so, if you buy the record, or the tape, then you *control* when you can hear it, when what you want is for it to be like luck, and like fate, and to zoom up and down the dial, looking for the song you want, hoping some station will play it—and the joy when it finally rotates around is so intense. You're not hearing it, you're overhearing it."

"On the other hand," she said, "if you own the tape, you show you've got some self-knowledge: you know what you like, you know how to make yourself happy, you're not just wandering in this welter of chance occurrences, passively hoping the disk jockey will come through. Maybe when you're a little kid you find yourself out on a balcony in the sun and you think, My oh my, this feels unexpectedly nice. But later on you think, I know that I will feel a particular kind of pleasure if I walk out onto this balcony and sit in that chair, and I wish to experience that pleasure now."

"Well, right, and so the reason I called this line was that the pleasures I'd sought out weren't doing it for me and there was this hope of luck, that I, that there would be a conversation . . ."

"You never said what it was about the Disney Tinker Bell exactly, at the video store."

"Well, in the scene I saw, and this is the first time I've seen any of this particular Disney by the way, and you have to remember that I'm in an altered state there in the movie store, with my three orange movies and my men's magazine in my briefcase, but in the scene, Tinker Bell zips around in a sprightly way, with lots of zings of the xylophone and little sparkly stars trailing her flight, and you think, right, typical fairy image, ho hum. And she's *tiny*, she's a tiny suburbanite, she's about five inches tall. This insubstantial, magical, cutely Walt Disneyish woman. But then this thing happens. She pauses in midair, and she looks down at herself, and she's got quite small breasts—"

"I thought you didn't like that word."

"You're right, but sometimes it seems right. Actually most of the time it's the right word. Anyway, she's got quite small breasts but quite *large* little hips, and *large* little thighs, and she's wearing this tiny little outfit that's torn or jaggedly cut and barely covers her, and she looks down at herself, a lovely little pouty face, and she puts her hands on her hips as if to measure them, and she shakes her head sadly—too wide, too wide. *Oh* that got me hot! This tiny sprite with *big hips*. And then a second later she gets caught in a dresser drawer among a lot of sewing things and she tries to fly out the keyhole but—nope, her hips are too wide, she gets stuck!"

"Sounds sizzling hot."

"It was."

"You remember *Gentlemen Prefer Blondes*, when Marilyn Monroe tries to squeeze through a porthole on a ship, but her hips are too wide?"

"I *don't* remember that. I better rent that."

"It would be funny if Tinker Bell inspired old Marilyn," she said. "You know, I found the Disney *Peter Pan* vaguely sexual, too."

"Well, yeah—J. M. Barrie was a fudgepacker from way back, and clearly some of that forbiddenness sneaks into every version."

"The girl floats around in her nightgown," she said.

"That interested me quite a bit. And she's *too old* to live in the room with the littler kids—I remember that. I must have been about twelve. I saw it with my friend Pamela, who I think has turned out to be a lesbian, bless her soul. We used to build tents in her bedroom and eat Saltines and read the medical encyclopedia together. It showed the dotted lines where the surgeon would cut cartilage from the ears if you were having an operation to make your ears flare out less. And at the end of each entry it would say, it was done in a question-and-answer format, it would say, 'When can marital relations be resumed?' And the answer always was four to six weeks. No matter where the dotted lines were, it seemed you could always resume marital relations after four to six weeks. I used to read the articles aloud to her. And once she read a whole romance novel aloud to me in one night. I fell asleep somewhere in the middle and woke up again later—Pamela was a little hoarse, but she was still reading. And once, maybe it was that same night, I told her a sexual fantasy I'd had a few times, in which I'm at a place where I'm told I have to take off all my clothes and get into this tube."

"Sorry, get into what?"

"This tube, a long tube," she said. "I slide in, feet first, and I begin moving down this very long tube, on some sort of slow current of oil. I'm sure you remember those water slides that you set up on the lawn, that destroyed the grass? This was not as fast-moving as that, much

41

slower-moving, but no friction, and in a luminous tube. As I went along these pairs of hands would enter the tube a little ahead of me, waving around blindly, looking for something to feel, and then my feet would brush under them, and they would try to grasp my ankles, but their fingers were dripping with oil, and as I moved forward they slid up my legs, holding me quite hard, but without friction because of the oil, and then they pressed down as my stomach went under them, and then they sort of turned to encounter my breasts, the two thumbs were almost touching, and they slid very slowly over my breasts, pushing them up, and believe me, in this fantasy I had very large heavy breasts, it took a long time for the hands to slide over them."

"Wow! What did old Pamela say when you told her that?"

"I finished describing it, and I asked her if she had thoughts like that and she said 'No!' in quite a shocked voice. She said, 'No! Tell me another.' You think maybe my tube was what turned her into a lesbian?"

"Well, it certainly would have turned me into a lesbian. But now—can you clarify one thing for me? Do you right now have the light on or off in the room you're in, the combination living room dining room?"

"I have it on. It's a table lamp. I could turn it off if you'd like."

"Perhaps that, perhaps that would . . ."

"Listen." There was a click.

"Now your silverware is glinting in the moonlight, right?" he said.

"I can't see it."

"Have you noticed that little juncture in movies, or I guess it's more in TV shows, when somebody has some pensive thought, or peaceful thought, close-up of her face, and then she reaches over and turns out the bedside light, click, but of course this is a movie set, with elaborate lights all over the place, so her turning that little switch has to coincide with the shutting off of major flows of current, *kashoonk*, and the problem then is that movie film doesn't work in the dark, so there has to be quite a high light level but with the impression of darkness, and so at the same instant the big imitation incandescent lamp lights are turned off, the imitation moonlight or streetlight lights have to come on outside the window, and yet there is often a problem, there is often a tiny millisecond delay while the filaments of the moonlight lights heat up and reach their peak, and so in this changeover you can see the second set of lights that are supposed to mean 'dark peaceful room' spread over the bed and the walls? Have you noticed that?"

"No," she said. "But it sounds very interesting and I promise I will look for it next time I watch TV."

"Do," he said. "Meanwhile you'll be glad to know that the real streetlight outside my window is beginning to come on. It's the most amazing effect. It doesn't come on all at once, it's nothing like what I just described. It comes on very very gradually, over about twenty minutes. It starts off in a very deep orange phase. I very seldom have *time* to watch it, of course, with my hectic schedule. But when I do, it really is quite beautiful. It's so gradual that you're not quite sure whether it's the light coming on and shining a little more brightly, or if the sky has darkened—of course it's both, but you can't tell which is overtaking the other, and then there's this moment, about five minutes from now, when the streetlight is exactly the same color as the sky, I mean exactly the same green-violet-yellow whatever, so that it seems as if there's a *hole* in the middle of the tree across the street, in the branches, where the sky, which is really the light on this side of the street, shows through."

There was a pause.

"Listen," she said. "This is getting expensive, at a dollar a minute or whatever it is."

"Ninety-five cents per half minute, I think."

"So give me your number and I'll call you back," she said.

"All right. But."

"Yes?"

"But then you'll have to turn your light on again to write my number down," he said.

"What do you mean? I have a good memory for numbers."

"Oh, I'm sure it's much better than mine. But what if in this one isolated case the number slips your mind?"

"Okay, to be safe I'll turn on the light and write it down."

"But what if you write it down wrong, just because this is such an unusual sort of occasion, and you reverse two numbers, the first time you've ever done it?"

"Sexual dyslexia."

"Right! Or what if you hang up and you get another Diet Coke and then you decide, no, this is crazy, I don't want to call him back? How do I know you won't just not call?"

"I'm going to call you back," she said. "I'm *enjoying* this. I'm going to call."

"Okay, but what if you do call, but because of the break, even that one-minute break, when we aren't connected, what if fate shifts, and we're suddenly awkward with each other, and we're never quite able to resume the intimacy that we seemed to hit so easily the first time?"

"All right, you convinced me. Don't give me your number."

"Really I think two dollars a minute is *cheap* for this. I need this. I'd spend twenty dollars a minute for this. And there isn't a time limit on this line, either—at least my ad says NO TIME LIMIT in big letters."

"Okay," she said.

"Okay, and in return for your indulgence, I'm going to try to do something with your heirlooms there, on your dining-room table. Let me see. All right, once there was a guy who had a big party, a big dinner party for a dozen

45

people, which really wasn't his style, but he did it anyway, and when all of his friends had left, he began cleaning up, feeling slightly depressed. He took the plates in, the glasses in, the cutlery in, man, he'd never seen the basket in his dishwasher so *stuffed* with silverware. He jammed the last fork in, but in his impatience to close the dishwasher door and go to bed, he didn't check that the fork was all the way in the basket, and as it happened it was not, because the forks were so tightly squeezed in there that he would have really had to work it down for it to stay put. This was one of the older-style dishwashers, and when that fork was tossed aloft by the first powerful spray of water up from the impeller, it fell, and it happened to fall so that it was caught dangling somehow between a plate and the little loop on the handle of a saucepan, with the points up, and the handle dangling far enough down that the sprayer in the bottom swung into it at full speed and notched it, and made it swing up again but not completely out of the way, and so it swung down into the path of the sprayer thing again and again, and got very messed up, and by the time this guy was able to get back to the kitchen and turn off the dishwasher, which sounded awful, the fork was badly injured. He dried the fork with a paper towel, and the rough places on the fork tore the paper, and that was too much for him, he almost felt like throwing the fork away, and he went to bed very dejected, wondering what the point of it all was. Okay? Now in this same city there was a jewelry

store, that some might say was a little bit too trendy, but
that was still a very nice place—they didn't sell diamonds
or emeralds or conventional big-ticket items like that, in
fact it was called 'Harvey's Semi-Precious,' after Harvey,
the owner—and mostly it sold artisan stuff and collecti-
bles. And *you* got a job there."

"I did?" she said.

"What happened was, you went to a program in a
university, and you got a masters in silversmithing, with
some postgraduate work in pendant mounting and bead
drilling, and you found that you had a very good eye, and
you really were able to make bracelets and earrings and
especially necklaces that looked good on people, not that
looked good in the display case, in fact sometimes your
work even looked a little strange, a little knobby and
unsure of itself in the display case, but on the human
form—divine. So you graduate from the program and it's
time to make a living, and you take your best work around
to various jewelry places, and you get a mixed reaction,
frankly, the world isn't quite ready for you, and finally
you take it to Harvey's Semi-Precious, which you've
avoided because in a way it's a little down-market—it
started as a head shop in fact, and Harvey's this fairly old
guy now with a big collection of fancy cigarette cases
from the twenties that you find saddens you, and he's got
what you might call an old-world smell, but you interview with him, and he seems nice, and he's very encour-
aging about your work, and you decide what the hay. But

the only stipulation is, if you work for Harvey, you have
to work in the store, in this small glass enclosure that
kind of projects from one of the windows so that people
walking by on the street can watch you work. You're a
little hesitant about that, but he draws the curtain open,
tells you to take a seat, and it's this nice little room, with
many many small wooden drawers that are handy on
either side, and a whole set of silversmithing tools that
are mounted on little spring clips, and a nice flame there,
a nice blue flame, with a yellow tip, and it really seems
very cozy, and yet of course visible from the street, and
so you start work. And Harvey could not be nicer—he
treats you with kindly irony, and when you make a piece
he especially likes, he is very appreciative. He sets up a
special display case for just your work in the store, and he
doesn't mind when you come in a little late. And over
the first few months you start doing this series of bracelets, simple elegant silver bracelets, which Harvey puts in
the case. Naturally many of the customers who wander
into the store are young men buying jewelry for women
they love, and they're uncertain, they want to be sure
they're right to buy that particular piece, and so Harvey
gets in the habit of poking his head through the curtain
and asking you, very hesitantly and politely, if you might
want to come out and show the prospective buyer what
the bracelet looks like on a real woman. And you find
this a trifle embarrassing, because, after all, you made
the piece, but you take off your welder's glasses and you

run your hands through your hair and there you are walking out into the store toward smiling Harvey and the open display case with the key in it, and this nervous man who's in a hurry to get something for his wife or mistress is standing there, and you extend your arm, and Harvey puts on the bracelet, and the man's mouth moves, and his checkbook falls open, and there, so easy, it's sold. You sell about ten, fifteen bracelets this way, and with this success, you start to get ambitious, and you design and make a necklace, a very simple necklace, but with three stones that Harvey's procured for you, a tiny chrysolite in the center, and then, on either side, two lovely lustrous pieces of unpolished strumulite, which are, as you know, fossilized drops of dinosaur ejaculate. Nothing could be more tasteful—you surprise yourself with how well it turns out—nothing you did in school equals this necklace. Harvey is in rapture—he holds it draped over his fingers, which are all dry and discolored from silver polish, and he just shakes his head, and you feel very happy, happy at having found your metier, and happy at having found as good a person to work for as Harvey. Well, so, the necklace is hung up in the display case, not in as prominent a position as you think it ought to be, perhaps, and Harvey insists on putting a very high price on it, too high to sell, you think, but Harvey is, for once, adamant. Some weeks go by, and you sell several other small pieces, a ring, some earrings, but the necklace does not sell. You're curious, you peep through the curtain and watch Harvey taking customers over to your case, and you notice that he seems to be avoiding calling attention to the very fine piece, he's distracting buyers when they comment on it. You realize, not without a certain pleasure, that Harvey is probably somewhat in love with you, though he's too gentle ever to raise the issue. He now averts his gaze whenever you extend your wrist to put on one of your bracelets for a customer. And you begin to sense that he doesn't want to sell the glorious strumulite necklace you made because he is afraid that when he does he's going to lose you. And you feel that he's probably right. He's started asking you if you're happy, if you have all the tools you need. There have been other jeweleresses in the window of Harvey's Semi-Precious in days gone by, of course, and they have all gone on to bigger things, bigger commissions, but none of them has gotten to Harvey the way you have, you suspect."

"I'm a little full of myself, aren't I?" she said.

"You are, yes, and yet you're uncertain too. And so one morning, you're in your glass enclosure working away, and you look up and there's this guy standing quite close to the glass, peering in at you. You nod, you're used to this, and he nods. He's wearing a suit, and he's carrying what looks to be a fork, wrapped in a piece of paper towel. He looks up at the sign over the shop and you hear him go in and you hear him talking to Harvey. Harvey sounds a bit testy. You hear him say, 'She can't take her time up with uncreative work like that.' Then the guy says something, a note of urgency in his voice. Harvey says, 'No, I'm not kidding, really, no.' And you pop your head out of the curtain. The two men look at you. Harvey goes, 'I'm trying to tell this gentleman that you're an artist and you are not able to do something like repair his fork. He doesn't want me to do the repair, he wants you to do it.' The guy in the suit looks embarrassed, he holds up his hands. You walk out into the shop. You take off your insulated soldering gloves and put them carelessly down on a display of rare campaign buttons. You're wearing a shirt with small green and black stars on it, and black pants, and black sneakers. You hold out your hand for the fork, the guy gives it to you. You say, 'An incident with the dishwasher?' and he nods yes. And you say, 'Harvey, it won't take me a second.' Harvey goes, 'Fine! Go ahead!' and sits down near the register, staring straight ahead. He's pissed. You say to the guy, 'I'll have it for you by noon.' And you go back into your area in the window. You take up the piece you've been working on. It's some kind of brooch, and it isn't turning out very well. You've lost your inspiration to some degree, since Harvey hasn't sold your best effort. You look at the fork sitting there, and then you become conscious of a presence outside the window, and you look up, and it's the same guy. You give him a questioning expression, and he moves his arms to say, 'Don't mind me.' But he doesn't walk away. You look down at

51

the brooch again, but you don't like it, you don't want Mr. Fork to see it and think of it as representative of your work. And so you set it aside and you clamp the injured fork in several delicate vises, and you put on your insulated gloves, and you start playing the flame of the torch over the nicked parts. Repair is Harvey's area, so you don't get much of a chance to do this, but you find now that in small doses it's a very satisfying and soothing activity. Naturally you can't restore the fork to mint condition—you melt the roughnesses until they subside, and what you're left with is a lovely irregular mottled very shiny surface. You're glad you have your dark welder's goggles on: you look up covertly, with just your eyes, not lifting your head, and you see the fork man standing there sort of *slumped*, looking at you do those things to his fork. He's melting, he's smitten, he's silversmitten. You plunge the fork into a tray of water. He smiles. He goes back into the shop. You come out of your enclosure. Harvey looks up. You hand the fork to Harvey and Harvey looks at it and says, 'Twelve dollars.' Mr. Fork pays the twelve dollars and takes the repair job and says thank-you to Harvey. Then he says, 'I was just curious how it was done. I'm sorry to have taken up her time.' And then he asks, 'You say she's an artist. Can you show me some things she's done?' Slowly, slowly Harvey walks over to the display case, unlocks it, sighs. The guy leans very close to the jewelry, his head is practically *in* the case. You're watching all this. You notice for the first time that he's got his hair in a kind of ponytail. And then he points to the necklace and he says, 'May I take a look at that?' Harvey looks at you, he's got this almost pleading look, but you don't say anything. So Harvey seems to decide something, and he says sadly, 'That's the best thing in the store.' And he unhooks it from its little mounts and he hands it to Mr. Forkman, who again looks closely at it, holds it up in the air. Harvey says, 'For a fiancée or something? What's her complexion, dark or light?' And Forkman vagues out, saying, 'I don't really know who it's for.' Again Harvey looks at you, and you don't say anything, and so Harvey swallows and he says, he almost whispers, 'Really you can't get a good sense of it unless you see it worn.' And the fork guy says, 'Gee, yeah, too bad.' And he asks what the stones are and Harvey tells him and the guy just nods. Finally Harvey, almost in exasperation, says, 'Look, *she* made it, she knows all about it, she'll tell you everything you want to know, I'm going to get a bite to eat.' He turns to you and says, 'Show him the piece, all right?' He grabs his jacket and goes out, pulling the door shut with unusual force, so that the sign saying OPEN flips down to say CLOSED. And so . . .''

"Mm-hmm?"

"No, that's it, I shot my wad getting the two of you face-to-face."

"No! You're bailing out right there? Did you really shoot your wad, or you mean figuratively?"

"At the moment, my true wad could not be farther from shooting. It is *work* getting the two of you together. I feel that any second I'm going to misstep in telling this. It's very stressful."

"Now listen," she said. "Harvey leaves, slamming the door, so the sign says CLOSED, and I, me, I am left, abandoned right in the middle of things by Harvey, and I'm standing there in the shop with the taciturn and very rich guy Forky, Forky Pigtail, who's holding the necklace that I made in his big knuckly fingers. He sits down on a step stool, he looks down at the necklace, looks up at me. *What does he do?*"

"He says, 'I really do have to see what it looks like on someone before I know whether it's something I want.' And you look down at your shirt with the green and black stars and you sort of pluck at it and smile and say, 'I'm sorry, I'm not wearing the clothes for that piece. It's really an evening piece, for a low-cut dress.' With your finger you trace the ideal curve of the neckline of the dress. And Fork says, 'Then unbutton your shirt.' Well, what can you do? You unbutton the top three buttons of your shirt. With each button, you feel the fabric shift slightly against your collarbone. Fork stands up, letting the necklace dangle from his left hand, and, to your astonishment, he begins unbuttoning the buttons of his fly. Because of course he's a button-fly kind of guy. He unbuttons three buttons. The two of you are still about ten feet apart. You fold your shirt down, trying to make it follow the line of the dress that you should be wearing to wear the necklace, but looking down at yourself you see that you really need to undo one more button, and you dart a glance at him—has he reached the same conclusion? Oh no, he has! He is shaking his head. He says, 'I think really you'll need to go down one more in order to wear your necklace.' So you unbutton one more button, and he responds by unbuttoning the last button of his fly. He doesn't do anything, he doesn't reach in, you almost couldn't tell that his fly was undone, if it weren't for the fact that you've just seen him undo it. Oh, he is a bold bastard! What is he up to? He takes the necklace in both his hands, by both ends, and he shakes it, indicating for you to walk toward him, which you do. When you are standing close to him, he says, 'I think it'll be easier if you turn around. Then I'll be able to see the clasp.' So you turn around, and you see this necklace, your own handiwork, descend very slowly in front of your face, and you feel the dangly elements just touch your skin and you try to hold your shirt so it doesn't get in the way, but instead of doing the clasp, he lowers the necklace further and lets it accommodate itself to your breasts, and you hear him say, thoughtfully, 'Hmm, no, I really think the shirt has to come off entirely before I can evaluate this necklace. The green and black stars clash with the stones.' So you unbutton the shirt completely and let it fall off your arms. You're wearing a black cotton undershirty thing, with very thin shoulder straps. Very gently he drags your piece of jewelry up again, against you, and then finally he fastens it, holding the ends away from your neck so that his hands hardly touch you. You look down at it. It's hard to tell, but you think it looks kind of beautiful. Your nipples are visible through the black material. He's silent behind you. You say, 'Don't you want to see it now?' But he says, 'Wait, let me just do something.' And you hear a slight scrape of the step stool against the floor, and you hear his shoes on the steps, and then you hear some rustling, and then a very soft rhythmic sound, the sound of the sleeve of his suit jacket making repeated contact with one side of the jacket itself, and, as the speed of the rhythm increases slightly, you hear every once in a while a little sort of *plick* or *click*, a wet little sound, and you know exactly what he's doing, and you hear his voice, with a bit of strain in it, say, 'I think I'm ready to see it now.' And you turn, and there he is, on the top step of this little stool, with his cock and both balls pulled out of his pants, and with each pull he makes on his cock you can see the skin pull up slightly on his balls. I mean is this guy for real? And you touch your shoulders with your hands, and you pull the straps of your black undershirt down, and you pull it down around your waist, so your breasts are right there, out, and now you take hold of your breasts, your frans, and you lift them, so that each of the two side stones of your necklace touches a nipple, and by moving your breasts back and forth, you move your nipples, which are hard, back and forth under the two cool dangly stones, and you see him stroking faster and faster, he's starting to get the about-to-come expression, and you smile at him and move a step closer, so your breasts and your silver necklace and your collarbone are ready for him, and then you look straight at him and you say, 'Well, what do you think? Do you like it? As you see, it's really an evening piece.' And then, stroking very fast, he bends his legs slightly and then straightens them and he goes 'Ooh!' and then he comes in a hot mess all over your art."

There was a pause. She said, "Does he buy the necklace or does he just take his fixed fork and go home?"

"I don't know. I assume he takes the paper towel that he'd wrapped his fork in and uses it to wipe you off and wipe off your necklace and then he buys it and gives it to you."

"That's good. He sounds like an honorable sort. A bit precipitate maybe. Um—would you excuse me for a second?"

"Sure."

"I just—my mouth's dry—I want to get some more—"

"Sure," he said.

There was a long pause. She returned.

"It's funny that you cast me as an arts-and-craftsy type," she said.

"Not aggressively arts-and-craftsy. Are you?"

"Well, no. I'm really not, I don't think. Do you have a ponytail?" she asked.

"No."

"Then do you have an old-world smell?"

"I don't think that would be the word for it."

"I wonder what your smell is."

"I've been told I smell like a Conté crayon," he said.

"Hm."

"Or I guess it was that I smelled like what a Conté crayon would smell like if it had a smell."

"Well, that's good to know," she said. "Of course I have no idea what you're talking about. But no, you know what your story reminded me of, when I was in the kitchen just now?"

"What?"

"I was in a museum in Rome with my mother, and we passed a statue that had all these discolorations on it, a nice statue of a woman, and my mother pointed to a sort of mottled area and she shook her head and said, 'You see? It's so realistic that men feel they have to . . .' She didn't explain. And I don't know now if she was serious or not. I was—I guess I was eighteen. I thought, oh, okay, in churches in Italy, people wear down the toes of the statues of popes by touching them so much, and in museums in Italy, men come on the statues of women."

"Yes," he said, "I think I do remember coming on that statue. It's all a blur, though. There were so many statues in those years."

"Do you, as they say, like to travel?" she asked.

"You mean get in a plane and fly somewhere for recreation? No. I've never been to Rome. I spend my vacation money in more important ways."

"Like this call."

"That's right. Now tell me, though, really, when your mother pointed out that statue, was it faintly arousing?"

"I don't think it really was," she said. "It was just interesting, an interesting sexual fact, like something in Ripley's. I'm not, by the way, to get back to *your* story for a second, I'm not wearing a black undershirt under my shirt."

"What are you wearing under your shirt?"

"A bra."

"What kind of bra?"

"A nothing bra. A normal, white bra bra."

"Ooo!"

"It's shrunk slightly in the wash but it was my last clean one."

"It's always impressive to me that bras have to be washed like other clothes. Does it clip on the front or on the back?"

"The back."

"Shouldn't it come off?"

"I don't think so," she said.

"Oh, I can hear in your voice the sound of you frowning and pulling in your chin to look down at them! Oh boy."

"Hah hah!"

"The idea of women looking down at their own breasts

drives me *nutso.* They do it while they're walking. Some walk with their arms sort of hovering in front of their breasts, or awkwardly crossed in front of them, or they pretend to hold the strap of their pocketbook so their hands are bent in front of them, or they pretend to be adjusting their watch, or their bracelets, and the fact that even fully clothed the helpless obviousness of their breasts is embarrassing to them drives me absolutely *nutso.*"

"They see you staring, with your eyes sproinging out of your skull, of course they're embarrassed."

"No, I'm very discreet. And this is only in certain moods, of course. Once I got into a wild state just standing at a bus stop. It was rush hour, and there were all these women driving to work, and they would drive by, and I would get this flash, this briefest of glimpses, of the wide shoulder strap of their safety belt crossing their breasts. That thick, densely woven material, pulling itself tight right between them. That's all I could see, hundreds of times, different colors of dresses, shirts, blouses, over and over, every bra size and Lycra-cotton balance imaginable, like frames of a movie. By the time the bus came, I was literally unsteady, I could barely get the fare in the machine. What's that noise?"

"Nothing. I was just changing the phone to the other ear."

"Oh," he said. "Did you see that thing about the Chinese kid who suffered an episode of spontaneous human combustion?"

"No."

"You really missed something. It was originally in one of the tabloids, I think, but I heard about it on the radio. You know about spontaneous human combustion, right?"

"I'm familiar with the general concept."

"All right, well this kid apparently spontaneously human combusted, but the combustion was confined to his genitals. Boom! He was very uncomfortable. But see, I understand perfectly how that could happen. I fear for my own genitals sometimes. I get so fricking horny . . . now there's another inadequate word . . . so porny, so gorny, so yorny . . . I get so *yorny* that I look down at my cock-and-balls unit, and it's like I could take the whole rigid assembly and start unscrewing it, around and around, and it would come off as one solid thing, like a cotterless crank on a bicycle, and I would hand it over to you to use as a dildo."

"Okay then, hand it over. Although I've never cottoned to dildos particularly. I used one once, to oblige someone, and I got a yeast infection. I think it was called a 'Mighty Mini Brute.' "

"That's a fair description of my . . . crank."

"I know what you mean, though. Sometimes I get the same way, so worked up. My clit gets hard and it feels like this discrete wedge item, like a piece of candy corn, and I feel as if I should put it in a little wooden box for safekeeping. I usually like to come in the shower."

"Mm! Shouldn't that bra come off, really?"

"No it really should not, and I'll tell you why. When I dither myself off . . . no, I don't want to tell you."

"Please, yes you do, please tell me, yes you do, please, right now."

"When I masturbate and I'm not in the shower, I need my breasts to be tended to, but, boo-hoo, there's nobody to tend to them, so what I *do* is I pull my bra down so that the edge of it catches under my nipples, and then they're all taken care of, and I can use both hands to tend to matters below."

"This is a miracle," he said.

"It's just a telephone conversation."

"It's a telephone conversation I want to have. I *love* the telephone."

"Well, I like it too," she said. "There's a power it has. My sister's little babe has a toy phone, which is white, with horses and pigs and ducks on the dial, and a blue receiver that has no weight to it at all, and I find there is an astonishing feeling of power when you pretend to be talking to someone on it. You cover the mouthpiece with your hand and you say in this dramatic whisper, 'Stevie, it's *Horton the Elephant* on the phone. He wants to speak to you!' and you hand it over to Stevie and his eyes get big and you and he both for that second believe that Horton the Elephant really is on the phone. And then you get *two* phones going. Stevie's on the white phone with the ducks and pigs, and I'm on the yellow phone with the wheels and the eyes that move when you pull it along the floor, and I ask how Stevie's doing and have a little conversation with him and then I say, 'Stevie, would you like to speak to *Paul*?' And Stevie says yes. Paul is a relative—this happened last time I was back home—and Paul, who's sitting right there, gets this startled look, his hand automatically flies up to take the tiny plastic phone that I'm handing to him, he interrupts whatever real conversation he's been having and he says, 'Hello?' and his smile is very complicated—he *almost believes*."

"That's right!" he said. "And here I am talking to you, and you truly are somewhere on the East Coast, and you're wearing a bra!"

"Amazing as it may seem. What other words do you have for the things I'm looking down at right now and admiring?"

"Other words for breasts? Frans is the main one. Sometimes . . . frannies. Frans, nans, and Kleins. And I never thought 'ass' fit. Sometimes I think of a woman's ass as a 'tock.' "

"So then it follows that she has a 'tockhole' as well?"

"I never pushed it that far."

"Kleins is strange. 'I'm squeezing my big fleshy Kleins'? You sure?"

"I don't know, I think Patsy Cline is a sexy name. I don't even know who she is."

"She's a singer."

"I know that much. Once I looked down the list of

Kleins in the phone book and found one with a woman's name spelled out, and God, it was everything I could not to call that number. In fact, I did call the number, and she answered, and I said, 'Oh gosh, I must have the wrong number.' And yet the Kleins I've known in real life haven't been surrounded by a mysterious sexual power."

"It's that telephone."

"Your last name isn't Klein?"

"No," she said. "But I will tell you something."

"What? What? What?"

"Occasionally when I'm just about to reach an orgasm I . . . I think of it as a 'Delgado.' "

"Think of what as a Delgado?" he asked.

"The erect male cock."

"Oh, oh. Sorry."

"It's because I was infatuated with a boy named Delgado in high school. So when you said something about, something about your 'sperm-dowel' earlier, I misheard for a second, and I felt this *rush* of blood—I thought you were using my secret word."

"Now see that is what I live for, for someone to tell me something like that. I need that to happen to me every minute, every second."

"That's an impossibility."

"I will feast on that revelation for weeks to come."

"It's a secret, though, so . . ."

"*Up*, it doesn't go beyond this conversation. Out here

we say everything, but in our lives, nothing. Out here you can tell me, just *request* me, to pull on the knot of my bathrobe until it falls open."

"What kind of bathrobe is it?"

"White terry cloth. And you can just tell me, you can just say, 'Jim, please lift the waistband of your gray underpants up to its extreme limit of stretch so that it clears your erection and then bring it around and hook it under your balls, and then take that *Juggs* magazine and use it to fan your overheated pop stand.' And you know what? I would do it."

"Well, yes, I could tell you to do all that, but I don't know, those are important decisions you maybe ought to make for yourself."

"And I could probably ask you to tell me anything about yourself and you will tell me."

"Maybe," she said.

"You told me the secret word you have for the adult male cock, anyway. Not for my cock, leave me out of it. For the one you think about *on your own*. See, see, this is what I need. I need to know secrets and have secrets and keep secrets. I need to be confided in. Each time you come alone and you don't tell anybody, that's a sexual secret. The event has taken place and only you know about it and you have ministered to yourself in exactly the way you wanted to and thought of exactly what you wanted to think about. And each of these thousands of times you have come alone constitutes a perfectly unique moment, with precisely this order of images and that fold of yourself being moved by your middle finger in just that way and that biting of lower lip with exactly that degree of force, all entirely private. I almost think that each one of the times a woman comes in private in her life has to continue to exist as a kind of sphere, a foot-and-a-half-wide sphere, in some ideal dimension, sort of like all the ovums you've got queued up in you, except these are . . . ovums of past orgasms, weird as that sounds, and I am this one viable spermazoid lurking around among them, and I would happily spend my life floating up to one after another of these unique orgasm-spheres and looking inside and I'd be able to watch you make yourself come that one time."

"I bet each one of these mystical spheres has a little window in it with a little Levelor blind that's down almost but not quite all the way, right, that you creep up to and peer into, am I right?"

"Exactly, as if it's a stylized cartoon bubble with a curved window drawn on it, and you're naked in there, strumming like there's no tomorrow. But no, actually it isn't like simple voyeurism, I don't think—it's holier or more reverent than that, because when I'm in that mood I don't want to exist. I don't mean I want to kill myself, I mean that I'm a man and a man is a watcher and a watcher disturbs the purity of the event, so I don't want to exist, I want to be faded away to almost nothing. And of course all other men are completely foreign, they aren't allowed in this at all. When I'm very aroused I almost hate all other men. Sometimes when there's a kissing scene in a movie, and the camera shows the actor and actress chomping away on each other's gums, *moy-ong*, *moyong*, and then there's this sudden folded-up piece of shaven male jaw skin, I feel a wave of disgust— what the fuck is he doing there, get him off the set! That's not even to mention the bestial idiots in porn movies: this nice woman donating her perfect self to these horrible lascivious dumbfucks, with their suggestive evil laughs, and their intent lustful expressions, and their singlemindedness, and their constant diverting of the conversation around to sex. Get *rid* of them. One time I was in a store at the dirty-magazine rack and it was a little congested there and I reached sort of over this guy's shoulder to get a copy of the magazine I wanted to look at—*E-Cup* or something—didn't touch him, just reached over him, and the guy half turned his head and said in this psychopathic voice, but very soft, he said, 'Stay away from me or I'll cut you up.' I said, 'Sorry, sorry, I was *just* trying to get the magazine!' And he said, 'Well just stay the fuck away from me, okay?' Now I'd never say that or threaten that but that guy's reaction, when you're at the magazine rack and you want to be the only one there, among all these lovely kindly wonderful naked women, is a reaction I can at least understand. These groups of buddies who go out and drink beer together at strip clubs—it's totally mystifying to me that they would want to do that, have male company."

"But women *like* men from time to time."

"I know that, I realize that, and that's how I trick myself into accepting men's existence: women often imagine men when they come, so men have a reason to exist. In fact, this secondary deductive twist allows me to get aroused by stuff that doesn't really arouse me, like for instance when you went into that catalog thing earlier about the row of male models in the warehouse with their cream horns popping out of their shorts, I could think to myself, okay, her arousal is supremely arousing to me, and this image she's describing is the source or current expression of her arousal, and I could imagine your face thinking of those images, and therefore I was able to make them somewhat arousing to me. Like the religious nut who embraces the devil because it shows his utter humility before God—except I don't go that far. Oh! I know what I meant to tell you."

"What?"

"You know you mentioned that friend of yours reading you a romance novel all night? Okay, this is a good example of what I'm talking about. I went into this used bookstore one time, just to browse around, called Bonnie's Books. But it wasn't really the kind of place I thought it was going to be, it had hardly any old books, what it had was recently published pre-enjoyed books. A de-facto library. Shelf after shelf of these things, big thick historical romances, super neatly shelved, sometimes five or six copies of the same book side by side, *Love's Hurry*, *Love's Eager Trial*, *Love's Tender Fender Bender*, all that kind of material, but even though there were multiple copies of these books, they weren't identical, because every one of them had been read. They looked *handled*. *All* of their pages were turned. And turned by whom? Turned by women. My heart started going. I had entered this enchanted glade. I took a historical romance off the shelf, and I felt as if I were lifting a towel that was still damp from a woman's shower. The intimacy of it! But it was long—no way I could ever read a book that long. So I put it back. There was a woman at the counter, maybe thirty-eight or forty, perhaps Bonnie herself. She'd read some of these books! I think I was the only one in the store—I knew she was aware of me—I'd smiled at her when I went in. I wanted her to *see me* looking at the historical romances. And then I went a little further up this one aisle, and I came to a huge trove of romance novels—hundreds and hundreds of them—all organized by the specific subseries, some of which are slightly softer core or harder core, you know, in some they're allowed to say 'he frisked his tongue over her navel' and some they can't. And I got to this set of red books, only about maybe fifty of them, called the Silhouette Desire series, and 'desire' is written in this luscious sloppy longhand, in a diagonal—*Desire*. Alarm bells started going off in my head, and I thought of going over to Bonnie and saying, 'Um, do you know those Silhouette Desire books? Can you tell me which title in that series is the most arousing of all of them, in your judgment?' But I could never have done that. And it didn't matter anyway, because hundreds of female orgasms could be *inferred* from the books themselves—you didn't need to harass any particular woman, you didn't need to invade anybody's privacy, you could just hold any copy and think of a woman holding it open with one hand, with her thumb and little finger. It was all there in the pliability and the thumbedness of the book itself—it practically shouted at you, 'I have been near a clit as it underwent two orgasms.' "

"So did you buy one of these Silhouette Desire books?" she asked. *"Love's Tender Gender Bender?"*

"Can you hold on for just a second? I have to get it."

"I guess so, sure."

There was a pause.

"It's called *Beginner's Luck*," he said, "by Dixie Browning, and it's singled out by the publisher as a quote 'Man of the Month' volume. *Not only* is it heavily thumbed, but the woman who owned it before I did spilled water or gin or something on it, so that it's all wavy. It's got a permanent wave. You can imagine."

"Whew."

"As I was driving home I was so stiff from owning this pre-enjoyed book that once when I was stopped at a stoplight and I saw a woman in my rearview mirror I made a very small clit-circling motion with my fingers on the roof of my car, despite the bird droppings up there— the idea that she might notice and understand what this motion meant made me feel faint with excitement—but she was expressionless. Anyway, I took the book home and read it, and you know what? It was good! Not only did it give me a partial erection on two occasions, I actually got tears in my eyes toward the end! It's about a man and a woman in a cabin in the woods. He's a klutzy scientist, she helps him get less klutzy and finally gets him to shave off his beard and it turns out that when he's cleaned up he's irresistible and despite being unschooled in the ways of love he is successful in bringing her to a fever pitch. Good stuff. I mean I probably won't reread it very soon, but when you think of some of the stuff that passes for highbrow these days, you've got to admire it for hanging back so humbly in the genre category. But never mind that. I finished the book, and I pictured the woman who owned the book finishing the book, with her normal flannel nightgown on—she switches out the light, she closes her eyes, she switches on the alarm—and then I turned the last page of the book, and there were more pages, there were four or five pages of promotion, up-coming titles, etcetera, and I turned to this one page. You ready? I'm going to read it to you. It says, 'You'll flip . . . your pages won't! Read paperbacks *hands-free* with BOOK MATE I. The perfect "mate" for all your ro-mance paperbacks. Traveling, vacationing, at work, in bed, studying, cooking, eating.' Did you hear that 'in bed' in the middle there? It's squirreled away in a non-sexual list, legitimized, like those gigantic massager wands that are always accompanied by catalog copy that talks about relieving aching muscles and lower back pain, when what we're all really talking about is women making themselves come in bed. What this Book Mate is is this rigid-backed thing to which you *strap* the book using this quote 'see-through strap.' There's nothing the book can do, it's powerless—it's strapped wide open—open for all the hungry eyes of the world to admire. The ad says, 'This wonderful invention makes reading a pure pleasure! Ingenious design holds paperback books OPEN and FLAT so even wind can't ruffle pages—leaves your hands free to do other things.' And *that*'s the page of this book *Beginner's Luck* that I finally masturbated to: the thought of a woman reading that this invention will leave her hands free to do other things, and the thought of her ordering it and then maybe holding the strapped-open book between her bent knees so she can read the crucial page of pleasure while she goes to town down there . . . needing to have both her hands free *to do other things* . . . ho *God!* The problem is, though, that you yourself almost certainly don't find any of this arousing."

"No, well," she said, "I find it mildly arousing, for the very reason you already said—it's something that's arousing to you."

"But there's the thing," he said. "If you only find it mildly arousing because I found it exceedingly arousing, then I have to cancel my strong arousal and replace it with mild arousal, since the degree of your arousal is the primary source of my arousal. And then, the problem is, you'll find it only infinitesimally arousing and I'll then have to discard it as a total turnoff. That's the problem."

"We have to find a middle way," she said.

"The middle way is for you to tell me the last thing you thought of that made you pay some attention to your candy corn."

"I liked the story you told about the jeweler pretty well."

"No no, before tonight. Whenever the last time was you made yourself come."

"Last night. I really don't remember. These are fleeting things."

"Oh, you *do* remember."

"I was in the shower."

"Wait a second. Okay. You were in the shower."

"What did you just do?" she asked.

"Nothing. My underpants were starting to bug me. Go on."

"I was in the shower, which is almost always the place I come best. In college there were very nice marble showers, with high showerheads, and the water, the shape of each *drop* of water, was exactly right, fat soothing generous drops, but billions of them. I came many many times in those showers."

"Public showers, you mean?"

"No no, private," she said. "This little high marble box, with a marble foyer. It was very loud, and sometimes when the water collected and flowed together down my arm and between my legs and then fell from there it made this almost *clacking* noise on the tile. The dorms were coed, so potentially there was a man from my hall in the next shower over, but that didn't interest me. I used to take showers at odd times of the day anyway, when the bathrooms were deserted. One-thirty in the afternoon. I'd go to class, and I'd start drawing in the margin of my notebook, and I'd draw a little curve, and I'd think, hm, a curve, and then I'd turn it into a breast, and I'd make it a bit larger, and then I'd make another one, and then I'd draw a pair of hands holding the breasts from behind—that was always an idea that interested me, that I'd be sitting in some class or auditorium, dimly lit, an architectural history lecture, with slides, and a person sitting behind me would reach his hands forward and take hold of my breasts, pulling me back against the chair. So by the time I'd drawn those hands and those large breasts I really had to come, and I'd walk briskly back to my brown marble shower. I read something about river gods that excited me, too. Really, back then I'd put out for any body of water at all—a pool or a bath or a pond, or an ocean. We rented a house on the Carolina coast for several summers, this was when I was in junior high school, and I'd go swimming in the ocean, and as soon as I was in the water I'd want to dither, I'd swim far out and I'd think of the tons and tons of water underneath my legs, but of course I couldn't because there were lots of people swimming, so I'd come in the shower—oh, and that was an especially good kind of shower too because it was outdoors, in this wooden shed, and I had this freezing cold bathing suit on, which I would take off *in the shower*, and because the suit was cold my nipples were erect, as in your wet T-shirt contest, and I was stripping in the warm shower water, I'd slowly strip off this cold bathing suit, *very* pleasant to have the warm mingle with the cold, so that sometimes I could feel cold rinsing down my legs and sometimes warm, and I could hold the suit open and let the water fill it so that warm was just pouring out around my legs, that was nice, so my skin was all confused and very aware of itself, with the steam rising—oh, and there was a little metal mirror, I guess it was a shaving mirror, in this shower enclosure, which would get steamed up, even though I was outside. It was on the left wall as you faced the showerhead, which in this case was quite low. And after I'd taken off my swimsuit I'd hang it up on the nail next to the shaving mirror, and the sight of it all crumpled and dangling there was exciting, because it implied my complete full nudity, and when the shaving mirror got steamed up, I used to draw a pair of breasts on it in the fog with my fingers. The glass was cold. I wanted to press my breasts against the mirror, but it was too high for that, but I imagined myself pressing my breasts against this little mirror, so first squeezing them together and then pressing them against the mirror, and I'd just seen something on TV about one-way mirrors, so I thought of men in the garden being able to see my breasts stuffed flat against the foggy mirror. Once I even brought in some lip gloss after my swim and spent a long time putting lip gloss around my nipples and soaping it off."

"God, car washes must have driven you wild."

"Car washes. I did like that one part at the end, where the felt flappers drag over you, but no, not really—it was very rare that my family took the car to the car wash. Almost never. Oh, but I do remember one thing I used to imagine—I imagined that I shared a ride back home from college with someone I didn't know, and we get caught in a terrible tropical monsoon of some kind, and his windshield wipers don't work, and so I have to go out on the hood of the car and take off my top and kneel there and hold on to the antenna and kind of sop my breasts over the windshield just so he can drive. Actually, that wasn't something I thought of very much, that was just a one-shot deal."

"There are strong evolutionary pressures on fantasies, aren't there?" he said. "If it doesn't work, and if it doesn't metamorphose itself into something that does work, it doesn't survive."

"Yeah, even in the buildup to one orgasm, it's a kind of bake-off. You think: two cocks, each one poking from under one of my armpits, sperm squirting from them? Yes or no. No. I'm a geometry teacher measuring boys' penis length? Yes or no. No. Am I a nurse at a fertility clinic and my job is to strip for clients who have difficulty coming and then suck their cocks and let their sperm drip from my tongue into a test tube? No. I'm in a dressing room and some native-Hawaiian security guard is watching me try on blue jeans over the video monitor? Ooh, maybe yes. In fact it's kind of like getting dressed for a party, and being unsure of what to wear right up to the last minute, and frantically trying on one image after another like clothes, not knowing which combination looks really *good*, and it's getting later and later, and then finally you pull out this wonderful dress, with some rich pattern, and you slip it on, and ah, you can come."

"Jesus. But what about if you're reading and the images are not under your control? Say maybe with a Book Mate thing holding the book open?"

"Hah hah! You mean with my hands free to *do other things*?"

"For instance, yes."

"Well, I have a whole system if I'm reading."

"Say you're reading your copy of *Forum*," he said.

"Right, what I do is I read a little of it, whatever it is, the story or the letter or the novel, to see whether it's something I do want to masturbate to or not. If it's something that looks promising, I read it all through very fast, to find out exactly what happens and locate the spot in it where I'm going to want to be coming, and what spots I'll want to skip because they're whatever—violent or boring or somehow irrelevant. Then I go back, not always to the beginning, but I backtrack, and the distance I backtrack from the point where I've scheduled my orgasm I have to gauge exactly, depending on how close to coming I think I am—so if I'm very close to coming I only go back a paragraph, but if it looks like it'll be a while I may even read the whole scene or the whole letter that's *before* the letter I'm interested in and then go on and read the letter I'm interested in. And sometimes I misjudge, and I start to get close to coming when the big moment of the story is still on the next page, and I have to race ahead looking for the words I need, or sometimes the opposite happens and I'm crowding up to the big moment of the story and my orgasm is dawdling, not all the precincts are reporting yet, and so I have to read the chosen come-sentence very slowly, syllable by syllable, 'up . . . and . . . down . . . on . . . his . . . fuck . . . pole . . .' "

"So if you walked into a room," he said, "and there was an armchair, and a table, and on one end of the table was a TV and a VCR and an X-rated tape, and at the other end of the table was some book of Victorian pornography, what would you choose?"

"The Victorian pornography, no question."

"That's incredible to me."

"You'd choose the tape, right?" she asked.

"That or possibly the armchair itself. Not the book."

"The classic opposition," she said.

"True, but no—actually, it's interesting. Because I've heard for so long about those studies that say that women like stories and men like pictures I've started to feel lately that stories *represent* women and are therefore sexually charged for me, and in fact that's what got me so hot at Bonnie's Books that time, the idea that I was peeping in on a women's preserve. I think I *am* slowly starting to understand why in general people would prefer written porn. It gives your brain a vaginal orgasm rather than a clitoral orgasm, so to speak, whatever that means. I read one story in some men's magazine once, years ago, in the first person, written by a woman, or probably not, but written at least with the pretense that a woman was telling the story, about a sixteen-year-old girl who goes swimming in a neighbor's pool and of course her frans are still somewhat new and unfamiliar to her, and she'd forgotten that her top from last year was flimsy and inadequate to the demands that were made on it, and presto it comes off after she's swum a lap, and she's *so* embarrassed and apologetic, but Mr. Grunthole reassures her that she needn't be ashamed, he doesn't mind if she swims without her top, and so on and so on, and even though it was a totally conventional and undistinguished story, the fact that it was written in the voice of this girl, so I could peep in on her mixed feelings when her top came off, did give me a huge . . . an unexpectedly large return on my investment. I guess insofar as verbal pornography records thoughts rather than exclusively images, or at least surrounds all images with thoughts, or something, it can be the hottest medium of all. Telepathy on a budget. But still honestly I need the images. For instance of you there

79

in the shower. I mean, when you come are your legs slightly apart?"

"Yes."

"And do you have one of those legendary Water Pik shower-massage showerheads?"

"I do, but I don't use it with any of the special settings. It was installed already when I moved in. It's useful for cleaning the tub. But when I'm—I don't hold it or put it between my legs or anything, I just treat it as a regular showerhead. What I do is . . ."

"Yes?"

"When I start to come?"

"Yes?"

"I—"

"Yes?"

"I open my mouth and let it fill with water. The feeling of the water overflowing my mouth . . . You there?"

"*Don't* stop talking."

"But that's all," she said.

"You were in the shower, yesterday night, and the water was coursing onto your face and falling down from one part of you to another, like balls in a pinball machine, and your eyes were closed. What was in your mind? Oh I'd like to . . ."

"Excuse me? You're murmuring."

"I said I'd like to *clk*," he said.

"*What?*"

"Sorry, I occasionally have a problem with involuntary swallowing. I said I'd like to . . . put my hands on your thighs, very high up, and hold them apart and cover your whole mound with my mouth and just breathe on you, through the fabric of your underpants."

"Ooch."

"Are your legs apart right now?"

"They're crossed at the ankle on the coffee table."

"That will have to do," he said. "Tell me what was in your mind in the shower last night."

"I honestly don't think I remember. And anyway the things I think of go by so fast. And it's not like all I do is come and come. Very often in the shower I remember some embarrassing moment, or some dumb thing I've said, and I curse it out, I say, 'Get away from me, stinker.' For instance, I might remember this time after I'd come back from a party when I was quite drunk, so drunk that I started to feel that I was going to be sick, but this person was in my bathroom, washing their face, brushing their teeth, humming happily away, and I moaned, I was leaning against the door, I knocked politely, I made these feeble scrabbling sounds, but this person had used the hook and eye on the inside because the latch didn't work on that door, and he was just too pleased with the world to hear me, or thought I was joking, saying hello by knocking, and so I was sick on my own bathroom door."

"Oh, terrible."

"Sorry to be gross. Fortunately it was just the usual fruit punch. He was very nice, he cleaned me up, he cleaned my door up, he took off my clothes and put me in a nightgown. Then of course later he drops me abruptly because I tell him to put his pen in his back pocket. But so, in the shower, the memory of that kind of thing will hit me and I swear at it to make it go away."

"I understand completely. 'Git out of my shower! Go on!' "

"Yeah, yeah. And I wash, too, in the shower. And I think of all the things I have to do. So the coming is just one item on the list. It's not as if my life is wholly absorbed with it."

"Oh yeah, oh no, *I* know that. But—do you wash your hair before or after you come?"

"Usually I get the nuts and bolts out of the way, and then I test the waters to see whether I do want to come."

"What color is your hair?" he asked.

"It's a light brown. It's wavy. But it's fairly short. What color is yours?"

"It's black," he said. "So now tell me the things you have to do that you remembered last night in the shower."

"Oh, work things. Letters I should write—I should be writing them right now."

"No you should not."

"And I need to repaint the hall in my apartment. Ah, now I remember one of my sexual images from yesterday. The people before me put up this dreadful wallpaper, a kind of metallic wallpaper, with a design of a tree and a split-rail fence with a wagon wheel leaning on it, repeating over and over. *Bad*."

"Doesn't sound good."

"So I painted it when I moved in," she said. "I painted it a color called Paper Lantern—and I put on two coats. Someone said, 'You *know* that you're painting over metallic wallpaper, that's going to come through-hoo,' but I just couldn't make myself steam off all that old paper—the design would imprint itself in my psyche if I did that, it would rise up when I'm eighty years old, on my death bed. So I just painted it over, with two heavy coats. And the first year it was fine. But then we had that killer summer, and somehow the humidity sweated the metallic pattern back out, so that now you can make out the split-rail fence and the wagon wheel. But it's very faint. Now in fact I kind of like it. But I really should repaint it. So in the shower I had this image of painting the hall wall with a roller. What a waste of time. And then I thought, wait, I have the money, this time I'll hire people to paint it for me. And so three painters materialized, and then suddenly there was a large *hole* in the wall, about three feet off the floor, big enough so that I could fit through so that my legs were standing in the front hall and yet my head and upper body were in the living room. The hole was finished off and lined with sheepskin. I had nothing on. My hands were resting on two full paint cans. But the strange thing was the cans of paint were *warm*. There was one painter doing the living room, and the other two were doing the hall, where my lower body was. The painter I could see didn't seem to notice me. He was painting a wall with his back to me. The painters in the hall were using rollers, but they were those little detail rollers that you use for trim work, that are about three inches wide, the darlingest little rollers, that can go *everywhere*. Somehow I knew that one of these hall painters was mistakenly using the wrong color, it's a color I used in the living room, called Opulent Opal— apparently he'd taken the wrong can of paint from his truck. V*ery* careless. The other one was more conscientious—he was using the glossy Paper Lantern on the trim. These are Sherwin Williams's paint names, not mine, by the way. Anyway I called out, 'Ah, people, sirs? Please be sure to use the right color! There is a potential for confusion!' But they were talking and they didn't hear me. I could hear their sticky little rollers moving over that wall, *ssshp*, *ssshp*, *ssshp*, and they were having an idle conversation about the chick they saw on the lake that weekend riding in the back of an inboard motorboat in a pair of overalls with no top, so her tits flopped around behind the fasteners on the top flap, and then they made reference to the time on one job when one of them evidently quote 'ate out' the woman whose house they were painting and then she jerked him off onto a cracked slate hearthstone because she was paranoid about hurting the finish on the antique pine floors, and again I called out, as nicely as I could, 'Guys, please, make

sure you're painting the right colors!' and this time, instead of answering, one of them simply took his little
roller and got it very heavy with the semi-gloss Paper
Lantern and touched it to the right side, you know, the
. . . cheek, of my ass, and then I could feel him rolling
a stripe of paint right down my leg, over my calf, right
down to my Achilles tendon, and then rolling right back
up again. Like the seam of a pre-war stocking, except
wide. Then he worked the roller a little on the tray,
loading it up again, and he started on my other asscheek,
and went very deliberately down and up again. At first he
pressed quite lightly, so I could just barely feel the sod-
den fluff touching my skin on my upper thigh, and the
roller barely rolled, but then as he traveled down he
pressed harder, and some of the paint was squeezed from
the roller and dripped down my leg ahead of it. It was so
surprisingly warm. They'd had the paint cans in the back
of their truck, which was parked in the sun. When the
roller traveled over the backs of each of my knees it felt
very very nice. I felt myself arching myself up slightly,
like a cat who's being stroked. Meanwhile the third
painter, who was in the room that my head and my
upper self were in, was still blithely painting away, with
his back to me, so at least part of the job was moving
steadily forward. And I expected that the two of them in
the hall would now get back to work. But instead I felt a
pair of hands on each leg, and I was lifted for a moment,
and a paint can was slid under each of my feet. This was

not a particularly comfortable position. The rims of the paint cans hurt the balls of my feet slightly, and my legs were farther apart than I was used to standing, and the small of my back was pressing against the sheepskin lining of the hole in the wall. Not comfortable, but tolerable. And then I felt knuckles brush against the inside of my thighs—and I knew that the first hall roller was now beginning to paint a stripe of Paper Lantern that started just at the top of my pubic hair and rolled very slowly over my clit and the rest of it, like some heavy steady piece of road equipment, and then back over my clit. And at the same time, the other hall painter had loaded his roller with *the wrong paint*, the Opulent Opal, and he'd turned his roller sideways and he was now pushing a horizontal stripe over my ass, at first a light stripe, and then, on the return, a harder stripe, and then he rolled down in between, and I called out, 'No no, I'm telling you that's the wrong paint!' but he was very deliberately working the roller in the region of my, what shall we call it, my 'tockhole,' without seeming to hear me. Nontoxic paint, of course. And then I heard him put down the roller and he planted his hands high on my ass, holding my hips, and then he did an amazing thing. I felt his whole weight go on his hands, and on my back too, and he was apparently supporting himself like a gymnast, entirely on his hands, with his knees bent and his legs apart, and then a second later I felt this burning blunt nub press against my Opulent Opal tockhole, and then kind of urge itself a little ways in. I went, 'Yew!' and the painter in the living room turned in surprise and registered my existence for the first time. My hands were still planted on the cans of paint. And back in the hall, while the one gymnast painter was sinking himself unapologetically deep into my ass, I felt the other, the one who'd responsibly used the right kind of paint all along, now use his thumbs to hold my real . . . self open, my lips, and then I felt him slide slowly up my real hole. I said, 'Vvoo!' The living-room painter's eyes got big, and he studied my face with this look, like, 'What exercise tape has *this* lady been using?' I'm afraid that by now I was curling my upper lip with pleasure. My expression in fact was exactly the one I would have had if I had been biting open a condom packet with my teeth, that gnashy look, but the thing was—*there was no condom packet*. My painter loaded up his roller with wall paint, this was a warm neutral gray, and I mean warm, and he came over and he lay down on the floor underneath me, in the opposite direction, with his head touching the baseboard, so I could see his face and his paint-spattered glasses between my breasts, and he touched the roller to one of my nipples, and then rolled up between my breasts and down and over the other nipple, and as he was doing that he used his foot to pull another paint can into position, and then, still lying on his back, he lifted his hips up in the air with both boots resting on the can of paint sort of like a circus elephant on one of those little stools, you know? And he brought out his cock. The hall ass painter took this moment to remove his hands from my back, so that all his weight was directed through his thigh muscles and his cock into my ass, while at the same time the leg painter, who was standing, pulled almost all the way out of me and then he slid himself all the way back in so that I could feel the muscles of his legs hit against me, and I opened my mouth to say, 'Hooh!' which is I think almost certainly what I would say if all that was going on in my front hall, but of course as soon as I opened my mouth the cock of the man underneath me slid right inside, so all I could do was hum, and then all three of them came in me, one right after another, first the one in my mouth, surprisingly enough, then the one in my pussy, then finally the one in my ass."

"My *gracious*," he said. "And that's what you came to in the shower?"

"One of the things. I mean—it takes a while to describe it, but it was just a quick succession of images, among many. It takes me a good long time to come."

"Tell me others."

"Well, hm. The idea I actually finally came to was—it was really two ideas. Excuse me for a second."

There was a pause.

"What did you do?" he asked.

"I just got a towel so that I can have it whenever I need it to mop myself up. I don't want to come yet, and I seem to be getting awfully wet."

"Does that mean you've taken *off* your black pants and your sneakers?" he asked.

"Yes."

"Underpants?"

"No."

"And what color is the towel?"

"Green," she said.

"Where is it?"

"It's bunched in my hand, held in my unders where I need it. Now I've put it aside."

"Why don't you want to come yet? I won't object, you know."

"Because if I do, I'll crash, I'll want to stop talking to you this way, and I like talking to you this way. My clitoris is duplicitous: it always tries to trick me when I'm with someone, or when I'm alone, even—it says, 'Go on and come, Abby, no problem, you can come a second time in a few minutes, this feels real good, come on, don't be so conservative, I'm good for three or four!' But I know better. I'm not a multiple-orgasm sort of person. The *second* after I've come, no matter how foaming and frothing my level of arousal was, that's it, my clit is already starting to creep back into its clit-cloister and I'm thinking about other things. Two or three hours after that generally I'll top myself off in the shower, but not before."

"I see. Well then by all means keep that towel handy. I'm in for the long pull."

"Good. Where were we?"

"You were just about to tell me the exact thing that was in your mind when you came in the shower yesterday evening."

"Right, but do you mean the image that made me come, or do you mean the image that I had in my head *when* I came?"

"I—don't know."

"There's a big difference," she said. "I mean, the actual images that I have when I'm coming are things like, I don't know, elephant seals dozing on rocks, a carousel selection of greeting cards, a painting tightly wrapped in canvas, porch furniture—my brain is going so wild that there's no way to predict what sort of oddment will be there when all the flashbulbs go off. They're almost never sexual images. But before that, when I'm getting close, you mean, right?"

"I guess, yes."

"Yesterday I think there were two ideas, combined. I'm embarrassed."

"You're *embarrassed*, after just telling me about a triple-cock blowout?"

"But that's nothing, that's just a picture. The thing that made me come, I've acted on, to a degree, indirectly."

"I told you about buying the romance novel, didn't I?" he said. "I even told you about making obscene fingerings on the roof of my car. I've let my hair down!"

"Tell me what you look like erect."

"You mean from memory?"

"No."

"You mean undo my bathrobe etcetera?"

"Yes."

There was a pause.

"Welp. Um. What can I tell you?"

"Is it hard?"

"Yes."

"Was it already hard, or did you just make it hard?"

"It was somewhat hard, I just made it somewhat harder."

"Talk to me about it. Look at it and talk to me about it."

"Well, it's this thing. I don't know. Gee."

"Are you stroking it?"

"I'm—truthfully?"

"Yes."

"I'm pinching the underpeening skin in the fingers of my right hand, and I'm jostling my balls nervously with my left hand."

"Stroke it now, slowly," she said.

"All right. God, each time I pull on it, its muscle clenches. I mean, of course it's always done that, but now, with you telling me to look at it, this seems the most noteworthy feature, this clench."

"Go faster."

"Just for a second, though, right?"

"Right, no spontaneous human combustion yet."

"Right. Eee, that feels pretty good."

"I can hear your strumming in your voice, you nasty boy."

"Nastybation. I don't want to come, though. I'm going to stop."

"Prudent."

"Funny," he said. "When I was going fast, I pictured something that I've pictured for years and yet never noticed. I pictured doing an impossible thing—I thought that if I got too close to coming, I could somehow angle my leg and contort it so that I caught hold of my cock in my bent knee and squeezed it like a nut in a nutcracker until it stopped wanting to come."

"You're a strange case," she said. "It was fun getting imperious with you for a moment, though."

"Hah! Frightening, too. There are different rules on the telephone. You want to know what I actually thought of when you asked me to quote 'talk' to you about my cock? After the thrill and the terror had passed?"

"What?"

"This time I had a crush on a woman at work," he said. "She had beautiful long arms, of which she was very proud. I don't think she had a single dress with full sleeves. She had a hopeless thing for a man named Lee, who was a smugly flirtatious married guy, whom I personally disliked intensely. This woman knew I had a crush on her, in fact I used to send her a memo with a single asterisk in the middle of the page on the day after any night I'd masturbated thinking mainly about her. I don't know if she thought this was charming or not. On the whole I think it pleased her. I was not completely serious myself anyway. One time she even held her arms out in perplexity and said, 'What, no asterisk today?' She knew I loved her arms. I tried to get her to send me a memo with a pound sign on it the day after any night she had masturbated thinking about Lee, but she never did. One night I was working late and I started to need to jerk off. The place was absolutely deserted, it was a holiday weekend. I went past this woman's door, her name was Emily, and it was like I was passing a huge vulva, so big it had a desk inside, and I decided that what I should do is make an actual photocopy of my dick, in fact two copies, one before coming, one after, and leave these, along with an asterisk memo, on her desk."

"What did you hope to accomplish by doing that?"

"Well, I was very interested in having her *see* my cock, but of course I wasn't ever going to just flip it out in front of her, I needed some . . . distancing step, so that ho ho ho yes we're civilized adults here, it's all on paper. Well it's harder than you may think to make a copy of your dick. I know it's done in offices all the time, but I found it to be quite a project. Maybe if I'd been able to do some kind of *planche*, like your painter friend did on your . . . back, it would have been easy, but what I had to do was first try to get something akin to an erection standing at the copier of a deserted office on a holiday, I had to think of her seeing the copy of my cock on Monday, I had to think of her first thinking, Golly, what a nut, and then finding she had to stare uncontrollably at the specific image of my cock, *boyoing*, had to file that image away in a secret file folder where she filed away all my asterisk memos, and that some night, working late, she'd reach her long arms down to that drawer and bring out the asterisk file and go through the pages, asterisk after asterisk, until she found my cock. So I got hard, that was one hurdle. Then I had to place my cock down on the glass, but the way this copier is designed—I disliked this copier, by the way, that place is too cheap to lease a decent brand of copier—the way it's designed is that a normal eight-and-a-half-by-eleven piece of paper is oriented sideways in the middle of the glass between two marks, you know how that works, right?"

"Yes."

"So the problem then is that only a little sliver of the tip of my cock was going to make it in range of the footprint of a normal eight-and-a-half-by-eleven copy. There were ways I could straddle the machine, but this just seemed ludicrous. Finally I made a seventy-percent reduction copy of my dick, because the highest reduction setting used the whole area of the glass that my dick could reach, and so I captured something vaguely obscene-looking, even if the total overall scale was reduced. It looked like a little Quonset hut, halfway up the right side of the page. I wrote 70% REDUCTION on the copy. But obviously my plan to strum off hastily and then make the second copy had to be abandoned, because my dick wouldn't even begin to reach over the plastic strip between me and where the glass started when it was soft. But by now I was crazed with the idea of doing something for this woman that retained some shred of playfulness to it, so she could think to herself, All in fun, all in fun, and yet which conveyed the full force of the idea that I had been alone in that office that weekend with a huge erection, thinking of her. How do I give her that sense? Actually come *onto* the asterisk memo? That seemed crude. Do you think that would have crossed the line?"

"I think, yeah."

"I thought so. So instead what I did was—you remember making outlines of your hands in kindergarten? You held your hand still on the page and you traced around each finger, and all the little contours of your finger joints were captured, and you would go around a few times, and each time the pencil was at a slightly different angle, so you got this *aura* of your hand, that was so much more accurate than you could ever draw, and all you had to do was put in the fingernails and the little wrinkles on the backs of your fingers and you really had something? Once this girl traced my hand and I traced hers at the same time—I went very slowly, which triggered her ticklishness, and she laughed hard every time my pencil made it to the place between two of her fingers, but she was brave, she stayed put. Her name was Martha. I'm pleased to have remembered that! A teacher showed us how to make a turkey, using two hands superimposed. But that wasn't interesting, that was just a trick. It's the same with shadows: the beautiful thing isn't the alligators or bats you can make with your hands, the beautiful thing is the way the shadow image allows you to see so precisely what the outer contour of your own hand really looks like, those little bunches of flesh under each bent finger joint. Obviously this was what I had to do. So I closed the top of the copier and I took a blank piece of paper and again I concentrated on the idea of this woman's surprise and then transfixion when she saw my memo until I was hard again. I traced around my dick with a pen, holding myself in place with a finger and holding the pen straight up and down, and it was a very interesting sensation, not pleasurable, but very interesting, this cold pen. I went around about five times. And the great thing was, on paper, my dick looked really impressive. It looked like a *big dick*. Because of course the image you get is bigger all the way around by what, two pen radii, or one full pen diameter, so a good quarter of an inch. Much better than the copy, which as I said was this miniature sideways thatched farmhouse there in the right margin. So I wrote FULL-SCALE COCK TRACING, you know, 11:43 P.M., SUNDAY, NOVEMBER 24TH or whatever the date was. And I put the memo and the two pieces of artwork in her in box."

"You're kidding! Did somebody find them?"

"No no. I plucked them back out just before I left."

"Ah, okay."

"And I didn't send her any asterisk memos at all for about a month after that, which was highly unusual. She started giving me quizzical looks. Then one afternoon she came by and she asked me what was up. She said I wasn't my usual buoyant self. And I griped to her about a certain person at work, I lamented the fact that we were a second-rate company when we could be a first-rate company, the usual junk. And then I said, 'And there's something else.' She said, 'Well, what is it?' She knew it was about her. So, with this weird combination of reluctance and eagerness, I confessed to her that I'd made a copy of my cock and a cock tracing and that I'd put them in her in box late one night and then thought better of it. She said, 'Well, do you still have them?' I said, 'Gee, I think I do!' "

"You'd *kept* them? In a little file of your own?"

"Of course," he said. "After all that trouble? Plus this was in some way part of the whole thing, that I'd blurt out what I'd done and she'd ask to see and I'd have it on hand to show her."

"What did she say?"

"She said that the copied cock looked like a sonogram."

"That's it?"

"I'm telling you, she had it very bad for this Lee guy. I suggested that she could take the two pages if she wanted, for her reference. She said no thanks. We had lunch a week or so after that. She moaned about Lee, I listened sympathetically. Then I asked her, I couldn't help it, I asked her, I said, 'Never mind the photocopy,' I said, 'let me just ask you, was the cock tracing I showed you in any slight way arousing? Not right then in my office, to be sure, but later? Did you feel the slightest smidgin of arousal later?' And she gave me an indulgent look and she said, 'I'm really sorry, the pictures made me feel tender feelings for you, but they just really did *not* arouse me.' So that seemed conclusive."

"I would say so," she said.

"Yep. Yep. It wasn't. More happened."

"You mean you and she ended up getting together? What was her name?"

"Emily."

"That's right, you told me that. Well?"

"Well, we did spend an evening in my apartment," he said.

"The usual? You draped your best cummerbund over the lamp shade? She toasted you with the Koromex tube?"

"Something like that. But anyway, that was what I thought of when you asked me to look straight at my cock and talk about it. I have to say, that was one of the more unsettling questions I've been asked in my life."

"Would you like to know whether I would find a tracing of your cock arousing?"

"I would be curious about that, yes."

"I suppose it would depend on my mood. I might like to perform the tracing. If you traced my whole body, I might in exchange trace your pale Ramone . . . This mouthpiece I'm talking into? Of the telephone?"

"Yes?"

"It's like a sieve. It's like those little filters you put over the bathtub drain. Sometimes I think with the telephone that if I concentrate enough I could pour myself into it and I'd be turned into a mist and I would rematerialize in the room of the person I'm talking to. Is that too odd for you?"

"No, I think that sometimes," he said.

"But the interesting part," she said, "is that the trip itself would take a while. I think a lot about what it would feel like to be turned into some kind of conscious vapor. You know those trucks that come around on streets and grind up the brush on the curb? Those droning trucks? The guy throws a branch in, and it goes mmmmn-*yooonnnng*-mmmmmm, and all these tiny chips fly out of a high pipe? I think of that, except of course it wouldn't be painful—I think of the part where I'm just this spume of wood chips and pieces of leaves. Or you know what else? You remember those birds that were getting sucked into the jet engines? Sometimes I lie in bed at three or four in the morning and I imagine myself flying miles above the earth, very cold, and one of those black secret spy planes is up there with the huge round engines with

99

the spinning blades in it, the blades that look like the underside of mushrooms? The black plane's going very fast and I'm going very fast in the opposite direction and we intersect, and I fly right through one of those jet engines, and I exit as this long fog of blood. I'm miles long, and, because it's so cold, I'm crystalline. V*ery* long arms, you'll be pleased to hear. And then I recondense in bed, *sshhp*, as my short warm self. It must have something to do with my estrogen level. But that's what telephone travel would be like out there, I think. What am I saying, that's what it *is* like."

"Ooh, I love you, you tell me everything."

"I do seem to, don't I? It's very unlike me."

"It is?" he said. "God, I'm a compulsive confessor. But it's rare for me to cast my bread on the waters and have it return tenfold like this."

"Tell me the rest of what happened with your friend Emily."

"Why? No, no, it'll make me seem like too much of a type."

"You *are* a type," she said.

"You're right, I am."

"Don't feel bad about it—I am too. I just want to know what you're like when you're physically holding a woman. As opposed to calling up catalogs and strangers named Klein and that sort of thing, worthwhile pursuits though they may be. What did you and Emily end up doing?"

"I never actually held her, that's the first thing I'll say. So it's certainly going to disappoint you. It's a very common story, really, and I'm starting to want to impress you a little."

"Impress me with your candor—that seems to be your style."

"Well here's what happened, anyway," he said. "After I showed her my cock tracing and all that, it marked some kind of conclusion, and we were more reserved with each other. After all, what was there to say? I'd laid it right out on the table and she'd basically rejected me. But then there was a big good-bye party for somebody, and at it Lee flirted with her in his perky cool way. Boy I dislike the way he funnels peanuts into his mouth. He'll never see forty-eight again, and yet he throws his whole head back after he's been asked a question, drops in a hopperful of nuts, and then he answers the question while he's crunching. He tries to be sardonic eating peanuts! This is some TV convention that has gotten people in its clutches. Of course there are times when you are so full of something you want to say that you talk with your mouth full, I have no problem with that. What I find fault with is when you are deliberately using the act of talking with your mouth full to demonstrate just how totally relaxed and spontaneous you really are as a conversationalist. It's from growing up watching all those salted-snack commercials. Bugles. So I hate him, clearly, and he's at the party, and midway through, something bad happens between Emily and him, basically it's just that he makes it clear that he likes flirting with her but forget it, he's married. She tells me about it in the parking lot, she's near tears, and then she squats and holds on to the side mirror of my car and looks in it and she says, 'Well well—*I* look convincingly haggard.' That was her best line—in fact it probably makes her seem more vulnerable and lovable than she really is. That's not fair— she's very nice. So anyway, for the next full week I talked with her about Lee and talked with her about Lee, every possible angle on the situation, though I avoided telling her that I found him repulsive and childish, but otherwise we ventilated the topic fully. Finally I couldn't stand to talk about him anymore, and I said, 'Look, I have to ask your advice.' Because what she obviously needed was to have her mind off her own troubles. It was six, we were again leaving work. And somehow, by pure luck, this was the perfect exact *second* to ask her advice: she just about crumpled with relief and helpfulness, and she pointed to a café across the street and she said, 'Why don't we go in there?' So over a pair of up-signal caffè lattes, I told her the problem. I pulled out a piece of newspaper, and I unfolded it, and I looked at it, and I looked at her, and then I looked at it again, and then I told her that I was thinking of running a personals ad requesting something *very* specific. And she was politely curious about this, so I said, 'This is what I was thinking of saying,' and I handed it to her. It was the personals ad form, which I'd filled out. The ad went—this is going to disappoint you, though."

"I fully expect to be disappointed."

"Good. It said something like, 'You and me are sitting side by side on my couch, watching X-vid, not touching. You are short or tall, etc., you want me to see pleasure transform your features. I am SWM, 29.' "

"Was this an ad you really planned on running?"

"I think so, possibly. No, I probably never would have. I'd carried it around in my pocket for a while, it was starting to get that folded-for-a-long-time look."

"How did she react?"

"Emily said, 'Well, you can try, but I seriously doubt anyone's going to respond to that.' Which was quite true."

"Oh, I don't know."

"Even if she was wrong, I don't think I really wanted what I said I wanted. Meeting strangers, the awkwardness. It would take such a huge effort of will to get over the pure chit-chat socialness of the context. My erection would never survive it. What I really wanted was to hand that folded piece of newsprint to *Emily* and watch her read it. I said, 'What about if I took out the lame line about pleasure transforming their features?' And she said, 'But that's the only thing in it that's any good.' So I asked her, if she were me—I said, 'I know you're not me, but if you were me and you wanted to achieve this objective, how would you word it?' She said, 'Well, tell me what your objective really is, in your own words, so I get a better sense of it.' So I told her that I, well er um, I was interested, you know, in sitting on my couch, next to a woman, with an X-rated tape on, and the woman's looking only at the movie and I'm looking only at the movie, and she's well, um, masturbating, and as she starts to come she says, 'Look at my face,' and I look at her face, and she looks at the TV, and we both come. So she says, Emily says, 'All right, good, now we have something to work from.' She takes out a pen and starts drafting the ad on the place mat, she writes, 'You and me are sitting,' and she goes, 'Good, okay so far, nice colloquial note, that's fine.' I think she was really delighted not to be talking about Lee. And then she taps the pen on the place mat and she looks up at me and she says, 'No, look, you need to make the situation a lot clearer. You need to make her feel that it's all right. You need to talk about some kind of a blanket.' Out of the blue, a blanket! No, wait, I know what she said, *before* the blanket, she said something like, 'You need to make the woman reading it understand that some sense of what is right and fitting coexists alongside your depravities.' Not those exact words, but close to that. You believe it? *Then* she brings up this blanket. This was a whole new side to her. I said, 'All righty, what kind of blanket? You think we should specify the actual kind of blanket?' And she nods and goes, 'Yes, absolutely, the specific kind of blanket, the size, the thickness, the color, that's all they have to go on.' I said, 'Okay, well, what do you think? Army surplus green blanket, Mormon quilt, what?' She thought for a second, and then she said, she said, 'I think you should mention a blanket with a fringe.' I said, 'But I do not *have* a blanket with a fringe.' And she said, 'You're right, that's a problem.' And then she starts hitting me with all these questions. She goes, 'How far is the TV from the couch?' She'd never been to my apartment, of course. I said, 'Well it's on a rolling table, so there's no fixed distance, but then, the cable cord limits the range, so I guess it's probably about six feet from the couch.' She noted this down and she goes, 'Because the woman skimming these personals may need to know that. That little fact might be of the highest importance. Now, is the couch two pillows wide or three pillows wide or four pillows wide?' I said it was three pillows wide. She said, 'Like this?' and on the place mat she started drawing a couch and a TV, so I said, 'No no, like this,' and I sketched the layout of the room. Just the couch, the walls, the doors, the electrical outlets. I drew two stick figures with two arrows to indicate where they'd be sitting on the couch. She looked at this, and nodded, and said, 'Okay, now, the other thing is, you can't just say "X-vid." What tape will actually be playing when this is happening?' I said 'Wulp, it would be a pornographic movie of some sort, I guess I'd rent a bunch before she showed up, six or ten, and there'd be some trial and error.' She said, 'Well I just don't think you'll get a response with that kind of vagueness. You have to *commit* yourself to a situation.' And I said, 'But you know there are thousands upon thousands of dirty tapes.' She said, 'That's just it. Is it a classic that she may well have seen, or will it be something she probably hasn't seen? Will it be new to you or not? These little distinctions are *crucial*.' And she said, 'And also—if you specify a certain tape, then, you see, she reads the ad and she rents the tape and while she's watching it, the ad may become more and more interesting to her.' So I said, 'Golly, you're absolutely right. I do have to say which tape.' But I said, 'But I don't know which it should be. I know what tapes I like, but I don't know which particular tape would potentially be interesting to her.' And much to my surprise, she had a suggestion. She said, 'Let me make a suggestion. A dubbed tape. A foreign dubbed tape.' And she explained why. She said it's because you've got more layers—you've got the graphic stuff going on, but you've got mouths saying Italian sex words or French sex words, and then American actors going ooh and ah, and usually the American actors who do the dubbing are somewhat better than the American actors who've got to both have sex *and* act. And no L.A. boudoir interiors, no L.A. fireplaces reflected in L.A. wineglasses, no Ron Jeremy. Again, that's not exactly what she said, but that was what she was getting at. And then she said, still in a very pragmatic way, she said, 'For instance, Atom Home Video distributes a few good dubbed ones.' So I clanked down my coffee and I said, 'Okay. I accept everything you say. I'll specify the couch size, I'll specify high-end dubbed Italian-import porno, but still I just don't trust myself to *buy the right blanket*. That's what worries me. And I see now that I really need the right blanket to complete this. Will you help me pick out a blanket?' And she said, 'Tonight?' And I said, 'Yeah it *has* to be tonight, it really does, because tomorrow I'll want to send in the ad, and as you say I have got to include the size, the color, everything, if I want this to work. I *need* your help with this.' And she said okay."

"What kind of blanket did you get?"

"We went to this discount place, kind of a seedy place, blinding fluorescence, in a strip right near where we work, and we went to the blanket department, and there were all these big blankets stuffed into clear plastic containers with snaps, some awful-looking, but some not so bad, and it was very strange, it was as if the two of us were a real couple shopping for a blanket. She poked around, looking at this and that, and I'd go, 'What about this?' and she'd feel it, make a judicious face, nod. But then, when she'd covered both aisles, she said, 'No, I just don't see any blanket with a fringe, I mean a real *fringe*. I think I better get back.' I said, 'No, we'll go to another store!' and she said, 'Nah, the good stores will be closing by the time we get there. If there'd been a decent fringe available here, I could have helped you with the selection, but I think you're on your own now.' I went nuts. I started really hunting through those blankets, I was ready to call the manager over and have him go in the back. And god damn it if I didn't find this little acrylic blanket, jammed behind on a high shelf, kind of a standard green-and-blue plaid thing, no beauty, let me tell you, but with a long thick twisted fringe. She looked at it, she touched it, and she blushed, and she said, 'This one will do.' So I marched right over to the register and bought it. There was a cardboard insert saying, you know, SEEDYCREST FIRST QUALITY ACRYLIC BLANKET, and there was this stock picture of a woman smilingly asleep under a blanket, and as we're waiting for the woman to enter in the SKU number Emily and I both looked at this picture, and I'm telling you, nothing, anywhere, was as obscene as that picture on the blanket insert."

"How much was it?"

"Ten bucks, something like that, I can't remember. On an impulse, I bought a *People* magazine, too. So then we went back to the car, and the great lucky thing was, I'd been able to park craftily not right in front of the discount store, but to one side, a little ways down—we were driving in my car—and I'd parked almost directly in front of this video spot. The place hadn't been too noticeable when we'd driven in, but now that it was darker it had the flashing lights on, video video video, it was the brightest thing in the whole mall. So I opened the door for her, and she got in, and I handed her the blanket in this enormous bag, and I said, 'Hang on, I'll be right back,' and I darted into the video place and went to the adult section that they had sequestered away and I started looking over the boxes. I was out of breath, and my senses were so hyper-alert, I was scanning the boxes for 'Atom' 'Atom' 'Atom.' I knew I had to get only one single film, the right film, which seemed impossible, but I could feel myself surging forward on this irresistible surge of luck, and I found a couple of 'Atom' productions among all the Caballero Controls and the Cal Vistas and all the other little companies, and I rented this thing called *Pleasure So Deep*. I mean the title *reeked* of translation, it was perfect. I signed up for membership, rented the movie, was back in the car in five minutes. Emily was there leafing calmly through the *People* magazine. She said, 'What did you get?' and I said, 'It's called *Pleasure So Deep*.' She made this little 'Oh!' and she said, 'And you're going to watch that tonight?' I said, 'Yes, I have to, I need to commit myself to a situation, you've totally convinced me.' And she said, 'Tell me again, so I have it clear in my mind. What you're advertising for is a woman who wants to sit on the couch next to you and watch this movie and masturbate, right?' She put her hand lightly on the box holding the tape. I said 'Yep' and she said, 'Just that, nothing else, only that, nothing beside that, right?' And I said, 'Yes, just that. And I think I really have a shot at formulating the ad that will find someone who wants to do that, thanks to you. You helped me pick out the right blanket, and I think now I've got the right tape . . .' Then I hesitated, and I said, 'I *think* I've got the right tape, but still—that's worrying me now. How will I know that the tape is really right, and which specific scenes on it are the ones . . . ?' By this time we'd pulled in the company parking lot right behind her car. She was either going to get out or not get out. I said, 'Look, I'm at sea. I don't know anything about imported sex movies. I really need your advice on this. I won't be able to judge on my own. I won't be certain.' And I looked at her, and she looked at me, and, remember, I'd spent *hours* listening to her think out loud about Lee, and she said, 'Okay.' So we went to my apartment."

"Was it a good movie?" she asked. "Were there any statues?"

"Statues? Ah, you mean *statues*? I don't know if it was set in Rome or not. It was about this woman who seemed to be managing some kind of counterfeiting operation that stored the fake money in caskets. In one scene she has sex with this guy who has a huge clownish yellow tie on with a U.S. dollar sign on it. Pointless, silly—but never mind, Emily was right, the fact that it was dubbed was outstandingly erotic. And the breasts really looked European somehow: not quite so corn-fed and symmetrical, but again maybe that was an illusion of the sound track."

"So you watched the movie, or you watched Emily? What was Emily wearing, by the way?"

"She was wearing a skirt, and a short-sleeved sweatery thing, I think it was dark red, some kind of dark red with thin vertical gold stripes. Lovely small, proud, elegant breasts—I mean in the sweater."

"And you were in a jacket and tie?"

"Yes. I let her into the apartment, and the way my apartment is laid out, there is a very short entryway with a kitchen that opens on the left, and then you're immediately in the living room—so she walked ahead of me into the living room, and even though I was careful not to turn on any lights in there, still, *there* was the couch against one wall and *there* was the VCR on a table against another wall, and it was as if there was this phosphorescent dotted line connecting the two things, they were linked, nothing else in the room counted, and I saw her turn quickly toward me so as not to face the living room quite yet, and she put down the bag with the blanket— oh, I forgot one other important thing that happened in the car. I parked the car in back of my apartment building, and I went around and opened the door for her, and she handed me the bag with the blanket and *People* magazine in it, and then she got out, and then—and for some reason this seemed exactly right—she held her arms out for me to hand her the blanket bag again. It had become somehow hers to carry. I held the tape, she held the blanket. Anyway, she put the bag down in the middle of the living room, and she said, 'So, will you give me the *grand tour*?' And the conventionality of 'grand tour'

111

showed how nervous she was, but she was one of those people who are improved by being nervous, you know?— who are nervous in a way that makes your detection of their nervousness seem like a privilege. So I showed her the kitchen, the bedroom, the bathroom—she nodded knowingly at the magnets on my refrigerator—beautifully nervous. I listed off what I could offer her to drink, and she said she wanted orange herb tea and she went in the bathroom. So I put two cups of orange herb tea in the microwave. Normally I make only one cup, of course, and I put it on two minutes, but I figured four minutes to handle the extra volume of water, but it was a bit too long, and the water was very hot. I walked out with the two teas and saw her again in the living room, with her back to me: she had been looking at the TV—it's just a dinky Malaysian TV, somehow everybody still thinks that if you have a VCR, that means you've got to have a TV worthy of it—but I don't know, I think maybe even the smallness was right for that evening. But anyway she slid her purse off her arm and put it on the rug next to an armchair on the wall farthest away from the couch, and took off her shoes and put them next to her purse— establishing a little separate non-couch locus for herself. I went into the bathroom for a second, and when I came out, she was sitting on the couch leafing through *People* in the dim light coming from the kitchen. I still hadn't turned on any of the lights in the living room, because it would have been so uncomfortable to have to turn them

off later. She half pretended to be startled out of reading
an article when I clicked the TV on, with no volume,
and she said something about Arsenio Hall. But the ir-
relevance of what she said made her smile, because she
was sitting on the couch, and now the TV was on, and
that tiny super high-pitched sound of electrically charged
picture-tube glass, that sound that you can sometimes
hear even if you're walking along the street, if windows
are open, that is the TV giving itself away, declaring
itself, even with the volume off, that sound that your ear
seems to be able to hear better and better in the evening,
or appreciate better, that means privacy and at-homeness
and closed curtains and secrecy too, because it's like
when you snuck downstairs at six in the morning to
watch *The Three Stooges* and kept the sound extremely
low so your parents wouldn't detect it, but you always
worried that even though super high-pitched sounds
don't carry well at all, you thought it might travel upstairs
and the knowledge that you were up and watching *The
Three Stooges* would trouble their dreams—*that* sound
was in the room with me and Emily, and even though it
was just faces at a press conference on C-SPAN, we knew
what it really meant. She pointed at her tea and she said,
'On second thought, could you maybe plop a little bour-
bon or something in this?' So I did. I put the tape in, and
the VCR made its little swallowing sound, and I turned
the sound up, and then there was, without even an FBI
warning or anything, there was the logo, this blue word

ATOM, with this wow-wow-wow-wow sine-wave kind of
music that focused in on a note while the word ATOM
focused too. There was a little stylized spirograph atom
even—it was kind of moving to see this symbol which
once meant progress and science fiction and chemistry
and then the evils of radiation, and now it just means
'Hey, you're going to have to take this sex film very
seriously, as seriously as anything that requires a linear
accelerator to discover, I mean you can pretend to laugh,
and think how funny and ridiculous, but you aren't really
going to laugh, because no matter how many times you
see X-rated filmed sex in your apartment, just by renting
a tape, it still will have the power to shock you a little bit,
it's still always miraculous, always a blessing.' And then
there was a preview. I handed her the controller and I
said, 'Fast-forward anytime something bores you.' I'd forgotten about previews—all that fast editing, without any
progression, and the sudden jolt of bouncing frans, then
a sudden come-shot. I remember once going to an arty
movie with Richard Dreyfuss in it, I think, a long time
ago, called *Inserts*, that had an X rating, and wasn't very
good, by the way, full of the grimness that films get into
when they try to make art out of porn, so uncheerful, but
the thing about the experience was that it was a legitimate movie, but because of the X rating, it was playing
in a porn theater, this was sometime in the seventies, and
I remember seeing a man and a woman walking up the
slight slope from the ticket booth ahead of me, holding

containers of popcorn, because the popcorn stand, which normally was completely shut down, had been reopened in honor of this legit, name-star film, and the couple went through the opening so they could hear the bad electronic music, and they turned the corner, and then bang, they were in the darkness of the theater looking out over all those seats during the previews, which were of course previews of standard porn films, five or six of them, so on the screen there was this gigantic shot of somebody like Brigitte Monet sucking a huge horizontal cock, with loud squelching noises, and electronic octaves thumping away, and I saw the woman stop and flinch and grab her date's arm and look at him pleadingly—'You told me it wasn't going to *be* this kind of thing!'—and her date made this awful horrified 'I'm sorry' face, and behind them I went 'Tut tut tut' in refined disapproval at what was on the screen, because I wanted both of them not to think they'd made a terrible mistake, I wanted her to still like him, I wanted women then, this was when I was maybe eighteen, to see why X-rated films were so wonderful, I still do in some ways, and it has happened, over the last fifteen years, with video, to a limited extent, though as you say you would still reach for the Victorian paperback if given the choice, and probably you are right—but I wanted to reassure this woman that it was okay, people like me were showing up at this theater, nonviolent normal intelligent men, it wasn't the end of civilization—I made the disapproving

sound even though the sight of the cocksucking wouldn't
have bothered *me* in the slightest if it were just me seeing
it: I felt her tentativeness, and I wanted, sort of like a real
estate agent who takes a special route to the house he's
showing that goes through the nicer, fancier streets, I
wanted her to be squired gently toward the graphic image
of a come-shot, and to have a good experience here, not
to leave disturbed by male tastes, the same feeling I have
sometimes when I see foreign tourists in some city I know
walking around bewildered in some downtown area, and
I can tell that they're disappointed, and I want to go up
to them and say, 'I know this is the standard guidebook
thing you are doing, but forget it, this isn't our city really,
go see this neighborhood and that neighborhood'—I
wanted chivalrously to save that woman from the giant
crude cock of the coming attraction, just the same way I
used to think when I was little of swimming up toward
the surface holding a woman in trouble and letting her
use my scuba mouthpiece, and carrying her up on the
boat and taking off her wet cold wetsuit and toweling her
off as she got her breath and shook her head at her close
call."

" 'Oh, thank you, Popeye, for saving me from that
large low-born cock!' "

"Exactly. Anyway—do you still want to hear this?"

"Yes."

"Okay. Anyway, there was the preview, which was for
some terrible-looking post-*Caligula* post-*Devil in Miss*

116

Jones kind of movie, with lots of gratuitous grotesquerie, stuff I hate, torchlit sets, dwarves, but in the midst of that stuff of course there were, bang, these shocking pure normal sex scenes, whose abruptness I felt through Emily, because Emily was my guest on my couch watching them. Then the preview was over, and the ATOM logo came on and focused itself again, and I looked over at her. She was looking straight at the TV—the light from the kitchen was behind her profile—and she had her legs crossed, and one of her forearms was resting on her stomach, and her tea was in her left hand. Her skirt was pleated. She looked so exceedingly *clothed*. She lifted the mug, and I could see her lips meet it—the water was still too hot, so she had to do one of those long inward sips that makes the liquid lift off from the surface into a tea aerosol, and her eyes narrowed when she felt the fine hot spray of it touch the tip of her tongue. And then the movie began—*Pleasure So Deep*. It starts with a maid who hears a tinkling bell and takes something on a tray to a man and they talk for a second and then she walks away."

"Have you rented this movie since then?" she asked.

"Twice. It's also one of the three I rented tonight, which I'm probably not going to watch. Much more fun telling it to you. Anyway, the maid walks away, and then this thin Europop electronic sex-music starts going, and then instantly: cut to half-naked woman and man with cock, with dubbed moans. The woman is in her late thirties maybe, very attractive, with her hair pinned back. Emily watched this for maybe a minute, and then she looked over at the windows and she said, 'Are you sure people can't see in?' I do have curtains, but I honestly wasn't sure if people could possibly see in or not, and my apartment is on the first floor, on the side of the building, so it was a legitimate concern, so I hopped up again and got my keys and said I'd be back in a second, and I went outside and tried to look in my windows, and it was surprisingly secure: not only could you not see Emily or anything in the room, you couldn't even tell the TV set was on, I guess because it's a small set. So I went back in and sat down, slightly out of breath, and told her that you couldn't see a *thing* from outside. She said, 'Great, thanks.' I said, 'What's happened so far?' and she said, in a slightly unnatural voice, 'The woman and her lover have been fucking in various ways.' It was the same scene, in fact—this Italian guy, whose name turns out to be Mario, has his amazingly long cock between her breasts—I remember seeing that image and immediately turning to Emily and watching her eyes: every time there was a cut, I could see her eyes make a tiny movement to find the center of gravity of the next image. Porn movies are almost always done with very repetitive cuts back and forth between two or three camera positions, so I knew what the images were and yet I could watch Emily's eyes: say the alternation was between a close-in shot of the woman's head bobbing as she was sucking the cock, and

then a farther-back shot showing that she was kneeling
on the bed holding her hair out of the way of the camera
and he was lying on his back, A B A B, and I could *see*
the mixture of colors change on Emily's iris, and I could
see it make these exact little adjustments. The miracle of
sight. She had an expression of very alert frowning
amused distaste. When that scene was over, I said, 'What
do you think so far?' I just wanted to hear her voice. And
she said, 'As it happens, I've seen this movie before,
about a year ago.' Then we watched maybe three sex
scenes silently. Maybe more. Once I asked some question like 'Is that one of the counterfeiters?' And she said,
'Yes.' Otherwise we were totally silent, while these hard-
working Europeans struggled and jacked and sucked and
moaned and came in English in front of us. The men
came, anyway. It's still a rarity to see a woman really
come on a video, as opposed to thrashing around. There
was more of the dimensionless electronic Europop music. After one giant come-shot Emily put her tea down
and took a deep breath and puffed out her cheeks and
smiled. I laughed with relief. I said, 'Is it as you remembered it?' And she said, 'I'm a little chilly.' So I un-
snapped the plastic cover of the blanket and unfolded this
big acrylic plaid thing and put it over her, but I did it
wrong, evidently, because she said, 'Could you turn it
this way?' and she showed me how she wanted it. So I
tucked her in with the fringe of the blanket running
under her neck. Then I sat down again, focused on the

movie, and again there was the jolt—you have a moment
of two fully clothed work friends in a living room adjusting a blanket, and I'm stuffing two of its corners behind
her shoulders, probably the first time I'd ever touched
both of Emily's shoulders at the same time, absolute
coziness, we should have been talking about the very first
birthday we could remember or something, and then we
turn to the TV and there are tits swinging around and a
woman's hairdo swinging around while she rises up and
down on some expressionless Eurodick and we're hearing
'Oh Mario Mario!' After a little while there were some
movings around under the blanket, and then it started to
shake, sort of. She didn't say anything, she didn't even
change her breathing, she was keeping it very steady. Her
mouth was closed. She said, 'Could you do me a favor
and hold the blanket for a second so it doesn't slide
down?' So I held it in place while she lifted her hips and
moved around some more, frowning. Her face was fairly
close to mine but we didn't have eye contact. Then her
panty hose appeared from under the bottom of the blanket, with her underpants still nested in it, and then her
feet disappeared again. She said, 'Thanks,' and took hold
of the top of the blanket. Again the slight fast movement
underneath. Her mouth opened slightly, and I could see
her tongue pushing against her lower teeth, and she made
these very subtle little movements with her lip—not
twitches, that sounds too obvious and uncontrolled, just
these very controlled barely perceptible sudden move-

ments, as if several times she were on the verge of saying something that began with the word 'you.' On the TV a woman was making her fist go up and down on a cock with her mouth slack. When a sex scene ended, Emily's blanket would stop. We got to the scene where the guy with the wide yellow tie with a dollar sign on it has sex with the heroine. She says something like, 'Don't play around, just fuck me,' and so he does. This scene really got to Emily, and she took the blanket in her teeth so she could have both hands free and yet have it over her, so now there were these loomings as her left hand moved back and forth between breasts, and the little circling rhythm was slightly less constrained."

"What were you doing?"

"Whenever we were in a sex scene, I mean in the middle of watching one, I would slip my hand under my belt and press on myself, through my underpants. When the sex scene was over, I took my hand out and rested it decorously on my leg. Anyway, this scene with the man with the yellow tie with the dollar signs really aroused her, and when it was over she took the blanket out of her teeth and wiped her mouth with the back of her right hand, spitting out some of the blanket fuzz, and in the TV light I could see that her two fingers were all shiny from stroking herself. We waited through the filler stuff, we didn't care about dialogue or cars driving or any of that, now we both wanted to see fucking, period. The next scene was two women and a man. Halfway through,

121

it threatened to be a lesbo scene, and I saw Emily's blanket vibrate with less conviction and then stop. She needed to see cocks at work. Fortunately it didn't turn out to be a lesbo scene—one of the women was content to strum quietly on the sidelines. Emily's blanket began moving fast. But this time she didn't have it in her teeth, it was loose over her, so her movements began to pull it down. I watched the fringe say good-bye to her throat, and began to travel slowly over her bunched-up sweater, and over the bunched-up bra under that, and then the individual fringe things fanned out and conformed to her breasts and slipped off them. The slow descent finally stopped at the waist of her skirt. I was a little hesitant to watch her directly now; I watched her more out of the corner of my eye: I saw her squeeze one nipple with a finger-do-the-walking kind of movement, and then her hand moved to the other breast. This was her left hand. And no oohs and ahs, everything quiet, just breathing, sometimes her mouth open slightly, sometimes closed. Once she pressed her lips together and bit them. Certain signs also made me think that at times she was biting the insides of both her cheeks. I could tell now exactly how her legs were positioned—they were somewhat apart, the blanket drooped between them, and the back of her hand was making the blanket move freely—but that wasn't the thing that got me. What got me was, her whole arm was now visible, her whole right arm, and the fringe intersected with it just at the wrist, which was arched, reaching down, circling, and the thing was that I could see her long beautiful forearm tendon pulling and pulling, controlling her fingers. I just kept watching this. Then the scene ended; I pulled my hand out of my pants, Emily crossed her arms over her breasts. She whistled a little, mock casually. Three wet fingers rested on her arm. We waited. More filler. The heroine goes into an office with two men we haven't seen before, both in business clothes. They think she is charging them with cheating her in the payment for the counterfeit money. She says something like 'Gentlemen, I'm talking about my own needs.' And suddenly two men with ties on are standing on either side of her, and she's sitting in a straight-back chair wearing white stockings, and she's sucking one and then the other. Emily whispered, *'That's* it,' and her hands both now slid under the fringe. And then she whispered, 'Do you want some blanket?' I said, 'Yes,' so she held on to her half so that it didn't slide off her any more and I pulled some of it over me, so we were both covered from the waist down. I undid my belt and pants and pushed off my clothes. We were both stroking ourselves, and I could feel against the back of my hand the blanket pulling with her little movements as I made mine. I sort of clamped the blanket against the top of my cock with my thumb so that I'd stay decent and yet have my left hand free, and I looked over at Emily's face, and watched her eyes traveling over those double-cock images, and I looked down at her breasts. I wanted to touch them, but I knew this would complicate things, it would have been a mistake. I could have come anytime. But suddenly the scene ended—one man suddenly comes on the woman's face and breasts, the other pulls out and comes on her bush, with strikingly white sperm. Emily wasn't fazed. She said, 'Do you mind if I rewind a little?' I said no, so she rewound it and replayed some of the two cocks. When it started playing, she said, kind of softly, 'I think I want to come to this scene.' I said, 'Okay.' But again the scene ended too quickly for her, and she had to rewind it a third time. This time, I just looked at her, she was flushed, her cheeks were shiny, she looked so trans-formed and sexual and elegant, and I looked down and both her hands were converging under the blanket, both wrists arched, so that her arms sort of pushed her breasts in from the sides, and I said, 'Can I touch your arm?' and she nodded, and I put my fingertips very lightly on the inside of her forearm, just above her wrist, and I felt her tendon going and going as she stroked herself, and this indirect feeling of being able to take the pulse of her masturbating was too much, I said, 'I think I'm going to come,' and I started to come into the blanket, and when the first guy in the movie came on the heroine, Emily closed her legs and started to come herself, and when the second guy came on the heroine, Emily was still com-ing, but not with any thrashing around, very focused, but I could hear the shaking of her legs slightly in her breath-ing. It was really a wonderful experience. She picked up her panty hose and after I'd stowed myself away she wrapped the blanket around herself and I escorted her to the bathroom, holding the spermy corner like a footman so that it wouldn't fall against her skirt. Then I drove her back to her car. We kissed ceremonially, and she said, 'Thanks, Mario.' I sent her an asterisk memo the next day. And that was it. A perfect evening, perfect."

"Not to be repeated, or to be repeated?"

"Not to be. A work friendship probably can't handle more than one evening of parallel blanket masturbation without things flying out of control. I think that's what Miss Manners would say, anyway. She did get over Lee—in fact, maybe *Pleasure So Deep* was what finally did it. She's now going out with an academic and seems very happy. I haven't told her that I've rented the movie twice since then on my own and relived that buildup. I was surprised to find that we'd actually only watched about half of it. And I also found, when I watched it through to the end, that it wasn't as good later on—the movie was only good because she'd seen it, so the parts she hadn't seen seemed flat. Well, not *flat*, there was some hot stuff, but I rewound and came to the scene where the woman says, 'I'm talking about my own needs' to the two men. Since we're being truthful with each other, since we're being truthful, I'll tell you that that evening with Emily was probably the best sexual experience I've had, or at least one of the elite few. The sound of her breathing while she was biting the inside of her cheeks! God! And the sight of that blanket slowly sliding off her. And when she put her knees together. And it's not like I haven't done normal stuff here and there. But I don't know, you slip inside, and that first moment is paradise, incomparable, but then you're there working away, and you can't *see* the clitoris properly, you can't really concentrate on what it feels like to hold her breasts, what they look like when they move, you're distracted, your brain is moving your hips, moving your torso, holding her soft hips—hey, it sounds good! But you know? When I come inside it feels mystical but muffled—it's as if I don't feel the perimeter of my cock anymore, because that's merged with her, it's melted away and all I feel is the technical interior conduit structure of the thing and the bulb of come swelling and all that—I lose a sense of outer boundaries. You know? Or do you prefer the physical presence of a cock?"

"Well," she said, "I mean, if one is in there, I'm not going to tell it to go away. But actually, it's funny, it's another little bit of clit-trickery. As I'm starting to get close to coming, and I'm with a man, I get this intense wish at a certain point to have him in me, but if I pull him up from what he's doing and guide him in, that first moment is great, but then my whole area becomes, as you say, distracted—my clitoris is suddenly in close conference with my vagina, and I'm out of the loop. I like to *think* about cocks in me, though. Also, yeah, I do unfortunately tend to get yeast complications from real sex, inside sex, the friction seems to cause them."

"Exactly! See that? Who cares about my cock? It'll fend for itself. We're talking about your orgasm. We're talking about your strummed orgasm, the joy of it, the triumph of it, the greatness of it. I think of that moment you described of you coming in the shower after swimming, with the hot and cold water, and it's like I can hold out my hands and something tremendous and valuable is being dropped in my arms to hold."

"A folded blanket," she said.

"That's it!"

"I think it's fair to say that you are interested in women masturbating," she said.

"Any woman masturbates anywhere, I want to know about it. No woman is anything but beautiful when she is masturbating. Any plainness or overweightness or boniness or even a character flaw, an ungenerousness or something, everything is part of the recipe of her particular transfiguration, everything bad is pressed out of her when she shuts her eyes tight and comes. There used to be a tiny ad that ran in a lot of men's magazines, a half-inch-high ad, that had a shot of a woman lying back with what seemed to be, and it was very hard to tell at that scale, but what seemed to be her two middle fingers inside herself, and the headline was, I LOVE TO MASTURBATE. I probably came fifty times to that little ad. I'd look through at the full-page shots, but then when I was almost there, I would find this ad. You were supposed to send money to Mrs. Somebody in Van Nuys, and she would send you six hot photos and a pair of panties.

Right, sure—I never sent off for them. But the ad was a tiny window onto something, onto an idea: because there *is* a Mrs. Somebody in Van Nuys, California, who *does* love to masturbate, there are lots of Mrs. Somebodys in fact, and she is not advertising herself in men's magazines, she isn't wasting her time with that, she is simply masturbating, right now, and that idea fills me with energy, it's all I need from life, the notion that women are masturbating, and I don't know when or where, but it's going on. One time I drove all night back from college my sophomore year, and I shared the ride with this girl who was on my hall in the dorm who had a car, and it started to *rain* this mysterious warm rain . . . no, but I really did share a ride with her, totally uneventful, but just this past year, ten years later, we had a sort of reunion of the people who'd been on that hall that year, because it had been kind of a funny nice group, and this same woman sat next to me at dinner and told me in a low voice at one point that on that all-night trip, at six in the morning, while I was driving, and she was supposed to be fast asleep, that she'd made herself 'comfortable' in the back seat, just as we were going past the big GE plant in Syracuse. I said, Thank you, thank you, thank you for telling me. Ten fucking *years* that secret orgasm of hers was accumulating interest. Sometimes I think of myself up in a satellite, and I'm looking down at America, or anywhere, really, but I usually imagine America, and all these little lights are blinking on and off, and each one represents a woman's orgasm. That's what 'simultaneous orgasm' should really mean—the awareness of all those women's orgasms simultaneously going on. Maybe the women who are reading while they come create a slightly different flare of infrared color than the ones who are imagining something or coming in their sleep. I see them all. There is the woman who put the anchovies on my pizza tonight, there is Jill at work, who I got the tights for, there is an overweight rural woman with greasy hair and a missing front tooth, but she doesn't care about keeping her lip down over the gap, it feels too good to care, there's nobody to feel self-conscious in front of and therefore she's beautiful, and there is the thruway woman who hands you your ticket, and there's Blair Brown coming, and Elizabeth McGovern, and that woman in the John Hughes movies, what's her name, with the lovely mouth, and Jeane Kirkpatrick, and the porn stars too, but off-camera, Keisha and Christy Canyon—all these flares. Maybe it's not a satellite, maybe it's really a big black spy plane I'm in, and what's this, you're up here too, flying toward my fan-jet, surprise surprise."

"All that is somewhat indiscriminate of you, you know. You're using me as a proxy for all women who are masturbating at this very moment."

"Well, that may have been the original motive for calling this number, but I have never *talked* like this to any woman before. You're right, though, I can see that the idea of me suspended ten miles up over a dark twinkling continent, taking in the totality of female orgasms, might seem a bit indiscriminate. The fact is, I *am* indiscriminate. If I had called this number, and there had been a woman of extremely limited intelligence who responded to my voice, like say that one woman, Carla, who was on the line after you first came on, and she and I had entered our private code numbers and been transferred together into this 'back room,' and if she'd come, if I could have talked her through coming, that would have been a wonderful privilege and I would have come too and I would have hung up after twenty minutes feeling great. But that's why talking to you seems like such a miraculous once-in-a-lifetime thing, because you are smart and funny and aroused and delightful—you are *not* representative. We're actually talking! If you come on this phone with me, it will be, as far as I'm concerned, it will be the top item on *Washington Week in Review*, it will be bigger than anything your bearded friend who eats the meatball subs has ever experienced, it will be really *something*, because you get it, you understand, you have a complicated response to things, and, I mean, an orgasm in a complicated mind is always more interesting than one in a simple mind—maybe that's not true, maybe sometimes a simple mind is made subtler and finer as it comes, since that's the most mental activity that's gone on in there for a while—but I mean an orgasm in an intelligent woman is like a volcano in a mountain with a city built on the slope—you feel the alternative opportunity cost of her orgasm, you feel the force of all the other perceptive things she could be thinking at that moment and is not thinking because she is coming, and they enrich it. You still there?"

"I'm just trying to feel my wrist tendon," she said, "to see what it might have felt like for you. Actually, you know, there is a little muscle high up on the *outside* of my forearm that is moving, almost at my elbow. That's the one that's more visible in my case. Feels kind of interesting."

"Ooh, don't say that or I'll shoot."

"Hah hah! I like a man who knows what he likes. Do you want to hear what I thought about when I came in the shower yesterday?"

"Yes."

"I'll tell you. No, I know what I'll tell you. First I'm going to tell you something else. First I'm going to tell you about how I masturbated in front of somebody. It's short."

"By all means, tell me."

"Shall I tell you every nasty thing that comes into my head?"

"Yes."

"I will then," she said. "We went to the circus. It's funny, it excites me quite a bit just to tell you that I'm going to tell you. Doing that is probably the best part. It's just like that moment when you're lumbering around on the bed to get into opposite directions to do sixty-nine, that feeling of parting my legs over a man's face, *before* you put your hands on my back and pull me down, and my legs remember the feeling from the last time, the feeling of being locked into a preset position that is right for human bodies to be in, like putting a different lens on a camera, turning it until it clicks."

"And I," he said, "would feel the mattress change its slope, first on one side of my head, and then the other, as the weight of one of your knees and then the other pressed into it, and I'd look up at you and open my mouth and I'd slide my hands over your ass with my fingers splayed and hold your ass and pull you down to my tongue."

"Kha."

There was a pause.

"You there?" he asked.

"Yes."

"Tell me about the circus."

"Okay. Excuse me. I'm going to have to get a fresh towel pretty soon. This guy took me to the circus."

"The guy with the fancy stereo?"

"Another guy," she said. "It wasn't Ringling Brothers, it was some smaller-scale South American circus, with lots of elephants, and lots of women in spangles riding the elephants. It was incredibly hot in the tent, and everything had this reddish tint, because the sun was bright enough outside to make it through some of the tent seams, and I was wearing shorts and a T-shirt but I was soaked, and so was Lawrence, who was also wearing shorts and a T-shirt, and so was everyone around us, including the performers. There was some Venezuelan act in which a woman spun hard balls around very fast on long strings while two men played percussion behind her, and the balls smacked against the floorboards in interesting rhythms around her legs, and she was *streaming* with sweat, and quite beautiful, but in a way that I thought was vaguely like me, and suddenly the two men would stop hitting the drums and she would freeze and make this kind of trilling scream, a beautiful strange wild sound. She was just covered with sweat, she looked really wild, and the two men behind her were exceedingly good-looking, wearing wide-brimmed black hats with chin straps, and I momentarily wanted to be her, and while they were taking their bows I adapted my time-tested striptease fantasy, and I thought that I was this woman in the black spangles, and I was spinning these balls very fast, faster than she could, so they were a blur, so fast that somehow, like in a cartoon fight when it's just a blur from which things, pieces of clothing, fly outward, somehow my whole outfit was torn in pieces from my body, and flung out into the audience, so that when the drumming stopped and I froze suddenly and made my trilling scream, I was totally naked, and all these pieces of my costume were still floating aloft in all directions, and each man who caught some damp shred of costume was overpowered and took his place in line to fuck me, and the two percussionists played the drums the whole time, and then they stopped drumming and naturally they fucked me too. But that's just an aside. The elephant acts were what were interesting. I've ridden on an elephant once or twice in my life, when I was small, and I remember touching the big lobes of its head, and let me tell you, the skin is not smooth, it's warm and dry and quite bristly—that's how I remember it, anyway. And these were not little elephants, these were big old elephants, with big tusks. Well, these women were sliding down the side of the elephants, riding on the elephants heads, with their legs between the elephants' eyes, and repeatedly pivoting around on their bottoms on the elephants' backs, and they were wearing flesh-colored stockings, or tights, so it was not skin to skin, but even so, those little leotards are cut extremely high in the back, and I really started to be concerned about their bottoms, about whether they were more uncomfortable than their smiles let on, and I started thinking about whether if *I* were dressed in a very high-cut leotard I would like the sensation of the elephant's dry living skin on my bottom, and then, during the beginning of the very last big elephant promenade, one of the women was riding on the elephant's back with one leg in the air, and as the elephant turned I saw this woman's bottom, and even through the tights I could see that it was in fact red! She was the main elephant woman, I think. Anyhow, for the big finale she rode around on this elephant's tusks for a minute or two, sat on his trunk, fine fine, all gracefully executed but surprisingly suggestive, and then she did this thing that really shocked me. She took hold of one of the tusks and one of the ears, or somehow swung herself up, and then she lifted one of her knees so that it went right *into* the elephant's mouth, and she waited for a second for the elephant to clamp on to it, and then she threw her head back, and arched her back, and spread her arms wide, so she was held in the air supported entirely by her knee, which was stuffed in the elephant's mouth! I mean, think about the saliva! Think about those elephant molars that are gently but firmly taking hold of your upper calf and your mid-thigh, while this elephant tongue is there lounging with its giant taste-buds against your knee! The elephant did a full turn while she was swooning like this. Then she got down and took a bow and patted the elephant under his eye."

"Wow, that's better than *King Kong*."

"Well *I* was impressed. Lawrence had come up with the idea of going to the circus—this was our very first time out, by the way, though I'd known him for a while—so he was careful not to be too impressed. While we were walking out to the car he said, 'I guess those elephants really respond to training.' He thought the elephant wasn't biting the woman's leg, but rather that its tongue was actually hooked under her knee. I was dubious, but it was an interesting idea. It was touching to see how pleased Lawrence was that I'd liked the circus. We were standing out by my car in the parking lot, just drenched with sweat, he was plucking at his shirt and squinting at me, and we were supposed to go to this clam-shack place and have an early dinner on a picnic table outside, and I just didn't want to do that. So I thought what the hell, and I said, 'You look hot. Why don't you come back to my apartment and you'll have a shower, and I'll have a shower and then I'll make some dinner and we'll do the clam shack another time, okay?' He agreed instantly—he was delighted to have the responsibility for the success of this date taken out of his hands. So he had a shower, and I happened to have a pair of very baggy shorts with an elastic waistband that fit him fine, and a big T-shirt, and then I had a shower, and I put on a pair of shorts and a dark red T-shirt, and everything was fine."

"But separate showers, no nudity."

"No, very chaste," she said.

"What was he doing when you got out of the shower?"

"He was peering inside a Venetian paperweight."

"Classic. He'd obviously heard your shower turn off, and then he'd stood there, holding the paperweight to his face for ten minutes, so that you would be sure to discover him in that casual pose, appreciating your trinket."

"Quite possible. Anyhow, he sat in the kitchen and we talked rather formally while I made a spiral kind of pasta and microwaved a packet of creamed chipped beef—this is a great dish, incidentally, Stouffer's creamed chipped beef over any kind of pasta noodles—I have it about once a week. Lawrence made an elaborate pretense of being impressed by this super easy recipe, and when I poured the spirals from the drainer into a bowl he came over to where I was standing and he said, 'I have to see this.' I was going to simply slice the packet of creamed chipped open and dump it over the spirals, which is what I normally do, but I was feeling sneaky, I'd just had a shower, and you know about me and showers, but I hadn't dithered, despite the *major* striptease fantasy I'd had at the circus, because obviously I couldn't, since a man was in my apartment, so I was feeling devious, and so I got out some olive oil and poured a little of it on the spirals, and he—he was definitely not in the know about cooking, and I'm certainly not much of a cook myself—but he said, 'So *that's* how you keep them from sticking and clumping.' I stirred them up, and they made an embarrassingly luscious sexy sound, and I just decided, fuck it, I've dressed this person, I'm feeding this person, I'm going to seduce this person, right now, today, so I said, I said, 'How very strange,' I said, 'I just remembered something I haven't thought of in years. I just remembered this kid in my junior high—you remind me of him in some ways—I just remembered his commenting that a certain girl must have used olive oil to put on her jeans.' Well, I saw Lawrence's little eyeballs roll at this. He said something obvious about extra virgin cold pressed and he snuffled out a nervous laugh and I thought, yes,

I am in charge here, I am going to see this person's penis get hard, and even though I have a smoldering yeast problem and so can't really have full-fledged sex I am going to have my way with this person somehow. It was probably that Venezuelan ball-twirling screamer that put me in that mood, now that I think back. I mean, I felt powerful and shrewd and effortlessly in control and everything else I usually don't feel. I cut open the packet of creamed chipped and I said, musingly, 'My grandmother was very careful about money—she always used to say that she was as tight as the bark on a tree. And I used to think about what that really would feel like, whether bark does feel tight to the inner wood of the tree. I used to put on my jeans and take them off, thinking about that.' Lawrence said, 'Really!' I said, 'Yeah, although actually I didn't like my jeans to be at all tight, even then. I liked them loose. The appeal was the rough fabric, and the rough stitching, very barklike, the appeal was of being in this sort of complete male embrace, but then when you took them off, being all smooth and curved.' Lawrence nodded seriously. So I said, making the leap, I said, 'And when I started getting my legs waxed, which is quite an expensive little procedure, I also thought of that phrase, *as tight as the bark on a tree*, when Leona, my waxer, began putting the little warm wax strips on my legs and letting them solidify for an instant and ripping them off.' I said, 'In fact, I just had my legs waxed yesterday.' Lawrence said, 'Is that right?' and I said, 'Yes, it's amazing

138

how much freer you feel after your legs are waxed—it's almost as if you've become physically more limber—you want to leap around, and make high kicks, cavort.' I waited for that to sink in and then I said, 'Leona's a tiny Ukrainian woman, and she makes this growly sound as she rips the strips of muslin and wax off, *rrr*, and when she's done both my legs and there's no more hurting, she rubs lotion into them, and it's a surprisingly sensual experience.' Lawrence was silent for a second and then he said, 'I'm inexperienced with depilatory techniques. I've never known anyone who had her legs waxed.' I said, 'Let's have dinner.' "

"What a tactician!"

"Not really. Anyhow, we had dinner, which was pretty tame. Lawrence had many virtues, he had a kind of bony broad-shoulderedness, and a deliberate way of blinking and looking at you when you spoke, and he was quite smart—he was a patent lawyer."

"Ah. Patent in*fringe*ment?"

"Yes indeed. But he had no conversational skills at all. He was putty in my hands. No, I'm actually making myself seem more completely sure of my powers than I felt—but still, I was pretty much in control. I started asking him how electrical things worked—you know, like what shortwave radio was, and how cordless telephones worked, and why it is that at drive-ins now you can hear the movie on the FM radio in your car. And he was full of interesting information, once you jump-started him

139

that way. But the thing was, I kept a faint racy undertone going in the conversation. For instance, I'd say, 'What do you think those ham-radio buffs really talked about? Do you think some of them were secretly gay, and they left their wives asleep and crept down to their finished basements in the middle of the night to have long conversations with *friends* in New Zealand or wherever?' He said, 'I suppose it's a possibility.' And about the drive-ins I said things like, 'It must be much more comfortable and *private* in drive-ins now, because you can close the window completely, you don't have that metal thing hanging there with the tinny sound, covered with yellow chipped paint, like a chaperone, you're not attached to anything around you, it's much more like being in a car on the expressway.' He said he didn't know exactly how drive-ins supplied the FM sound, because he hadn't been to a drive-in since he was eight years old, but he said that technically speaking it was an easy problem to solve, for instance there was a thing advertised in the back of *Popular Science* that picks up any sound in the room and broadcasts it to FM radios within several hundred yards, it's called a Bionic Mike Transmitter. I said, 'Ooo, a Bionic Mike Transmitter!' He said, 'Oh sure, it's this device that you can leave in this room, for instance, and it will broadcast any sound in the room to any nearby FM radio, if it's correctly tuned.' He said, 'Of course it's advertised with a big warning about how it's not meant for illegal surveillance. But probably that's what it's used for.' I said, 'You mean that whatever I did, whatever intimate private activity I engaged in, would be heard by the people swooshing by in the cars on the expressway?' He said, 'If they were tuned correctly, yes.' I said, 'Hmmm.' You see, my living room is on the second floor, about three hundred feet from a raised part of the expressway."

"In some eastern city," he said.

"That's right," she said.

"So what did Lawrence do when you expressed a keen interest in his description of the Bionic Mike Transducer?"

"Transmitter. He asked if he could have a fourth helping of creamed chipped beef. Then we were finished and I started to clear the table and he said, 'I'll wash up.' I said, 'No, forget it, I'll do it later,' but he said, 'No no really, I like washing up.' So I said fine, and he cleaned the kitchen, quite efficiently, while I told him the plot of *Dial M for Murder*, really lingering over the hot letter that's found on the body of the man with the pair of scissors in his back. You know? Lawrence listened carefully—he'd never seen the movie, if you can believe it. He said he didn't like black-and-white movies. I said, 'Fine, don't like them, *Dial M for Murder* is in color.' He said, 'Oh.' And then he said, 'Well, I think Hitchcock was a fairly sick individual anyway.' I said, 'You're probably right.' Then he dried his hands with a paper towel and turned toward me holding the glass bottle of olive oil and he said, 'Now, where does this go?' I said, 'Well, where would you like it to go?' And he said, 'I don't know.' So I said, 'Well sometimes, after I get my legs waxed, the day after, they're still a little tender, and I've found that olive oil really helps them feel better.' Which wasn't true, they feel fine the day after, but anyway."

"Erotic license."

"Exactly. He said, 'But that would be terribly messy!' I said, 'So I'll stand in the bathtub.' And he said, 'But won't it be cold and clammy?' So I turned the bottle of oil on its side and put it in the microwave for twenty seconds. He felt it and he shook his head and said, 'I think it needs a full minute.' So we leaned on the counter, looking at the microwave, while it heated the oil. When the five beeps beeped, Lawrence took it out, and we went to the bathroom together. I stood in the bathtub and pulled my shorts up high on my legs, and very solemnly he poured a little pool of olive oil on his fingers and rubbed it just above my knee."

"He was kneeling himself?"

"Yes. The bathtub wasn't really wet anymore—I mean it was still humid from both the showers, but we didn't have the water running or anything. He said, 'You're very smooth.' I said, 'Thank you.' A rather powerful smell of olive oil surrounded us, and I began to feel quite Mediterranean and Bacchic, and honestly somewhat like a mushroom being lightly sautéed. He stared at his hand going over my skin, blinking at it. I pulled the sides of my shorts up higher so he could do more of my thighs, and I said, 'Leona is very thorough. No follicle is left unmolested.' Then, whoops, I wondered whether that was maybe too kinky for him and whether he might think that I was trying to give him the idea that Leona had gone over the edge and waxed off all my pubic hair, horrifying thought, so I said, 'I mean, within limits.' He just kept on dolloping oil on his fingers and rubbing it in. After a while I turned around and held on to the showerhead and he did the backs of my legs. He wasn't artful at all, he didn't know how to knead the deep muscles, but I could feel the intelligence and interest in his fingers when they came to each new dry curve. His hands went right up underneath the bagginess of my shorts. I liked that. He didn't say anything. Once I think he cleared his throat. Finally he said, 'Okay, I think that's everything.' I turned around and looked down at him: he was sitting with his legs crossed, looking at my legs, very closely, really letting his eyes travel over them. He had curly hair—he needed a haircut, in fact. He had the top of the olive oil in one hand and the bottle in the other, and before he stood up he pressed the circle of the plastic top back and forth up the inside of both my legs, in a zigzag. Then he stood up and handed me the bottle. He was blushing. I smiled at him and I said, 'Are you suffering from any sticking or clumping?' And he said, 'Yeah, some.' So I pulled on the waistband of his shorts and poured about a tablespoonful of oil in there."

"No kidding!"

"Yes, well, he looked at me with shock. And I know I wouldn't have been able to do it if they hadn't really been my *own* shorts that I'd lent him. I said, 'I'm awfully sorry, I don't know what I was thinking. Take those off and I'll see if I have another pair.' So he marched that peculiar march that men do as they are taking off their pants. He was not erect by any means, but he wasn't dormant either. I said, 'Did the olive oil feel warm?' And he said, 'Yes.' So I said, 'Would you like some more?' and he said, 'Maybe.' So I held the mouth of the bottle right where his pubic hair bushed out, high on his cock, I mean near the base, not near the tip, because he was still drooping down, and I tipped it as if to pour it over him, but I didn't actually let any come out. I just held it there. And the expectation of the warmth of the oil made his cock rise a little. I tipped the bottle even more, so that the olive oil was right in the neck, ready to pour out, but still I didn't actually pour it. And his erection rose a little more, wanting the oil. It was like some kind of stage levitation. His hands were in little boyish fists at his sides. When he was almost horizontal, but still angling slightly downward, suddenly I poured the entire rest of the bottle over him, just *glug glug glug glug glug*, so that it flowed down its full cock length and fell with a buzzing sound onto the bathtub. And this was not a trivial amount of oil, this was about maybe a third of the bottle. The waste was itself exciting. It was like covering him in some amber glaze. He hurriedly moved his legs farther apart so he wouldn't get oil spatter on his feet. By the time there were only a few last drips falling from the bottle, he was totally, I mean totally, hard. And of course with this success I had second thoughts. I almost wanted him to leave right then so that I could come in the shower by myself. I stepped out of the tub and I said, 'Sorry, I got carried away. And the problem is, I have this darn yeast situation, so I can't really do anything with that magnificent thing, much as I'd like to.' He said, 'Ah, that's all right, I'll just go home and take care of that myself, that's no problem,' he said, 'but your *tub*, on the other hand, is a mess. Ask me to clean it and I will.' I said, 'Oh don't worry about that, it's just oil, it's nothing.' But he was on his own private trajectory, and he said, 'That's right, it's oil, plus I have to say the tub is not terribly clean to begin with.' I said, 'No no no, don't even think of it, really.' He picked up an old dry Rescue pad that was in a corner and he held it up and he said, 'Look, tell me to clean your tub.' He's standing there, a pantless patent lawyer, semi-erect, wearing my Danger Mouse T-shirt, holding the tiny curled-up green Rescue pad with a fierce expression. *He wanted to clean my tub.* I said, 'Well, great. Please do. Sure.' He asked for some Ajax, so I brought some from the kitchen, along with a folding chair so I could sit and watch. Well, this Lawrence turned out to be some kind of demon scrub-wizard. He hands me my bottles of shampoo, one by one. My tub is now naked! He squats in it, so that his testicles are practically gamboling in the giant teardrop of oil that's on the bottom, and he takes the Ajax and he taps its rim against the edge of the tub, all the way around, so that these *curtains* of pale blue powder fall down the sides, kind of an aurora borealis effect, and then he moistens his Rescue pad and he starts scrubbing and scrubbing, every curve, every seam, talk about circling motions, my lord! He did the place where the shampoo bottles had been, that I'd simply defined as a safe haven for mildew, he was in there, *grrr, grrrr*, twisting and jamming that little sponge. Not that my tub is filthy, it isn't, it's just not sparkling, and there *is* a faint rich smell of mildew or something vaguely biological, which I kind of like, because it's so closely associated by now with my private shower activity. But here I was watching this guy *in* my shower! He took down the Water Pik massage head and he rinsed off the parts he'd done, and he began to herd all the oil down the drain with hot water, and the oil and the Ajax had mixed and formed this awful stuff, like a *roux* first, and then when the water mixed in it became this yellow sort of foam, which didn't daunt him, he took care of it. And then he started scrubbing his way toward the fittings, using liberal amounts of Ajax alternating with hot water. He said, 'You don't worry about scratching, do you?' I said I didn't. So he gnarled around the cold-water tap and he gnarled around the hot-water tap and he circled fiercely around the clitty thing that controls the drain, and then when the whole rest of the tub was absolutely *gleaming*, he went to the drain itself—he set aside the filter thing, and he reached two fingers way in, and he pulled out this revolting slime locket and splapped it against the side of the tub, and then he really went to work on that drain, around and around the rim of chrome, and deeper, right down to those dark crossbars, that I'd never gotten to, he worked the scrubber sponge in there, *grrr*, more Ajax, more circling, more hot water. I mean I was in a transport!"

"I bet."

"Then I held out the trash can, and he threw out the drain slime and the Rescue pad, and he rinsed his hands, and he stood, and in the midst of this newly cleaned tub he started to rinse off his cock and his legs, where a little oil had fallen, and I watched the water go over him, I watched the way the even spray of the showerhead in his hand made all the hairs on his legs into these perfect perfect rows, like some ideal crop, and he was quite hairy, and so I slipped off my shorts and unders and sat on the far end of the bathtub and propped my left foot against a washcloth handle and I hung my right leg out over the edge of the bathtub, so I was wide open, and I said, 'I'm a bit rank, too, do me,' so he started playing the water over my legs and then directly on my . . . femalia, and I held my lips open so that he could see my inner wishbone, and the drops of water exploding on it, and as he sprayed me, he began to get hard again. But I can't come with just water, so I started strumming myself, while he sprayed my hand, which was a lovely feeling, and I held out my left hand and he maneuvered closer to me and I took hold of his cock and tried to begin to jerk it off, but I didn't do very well, because my own finger on my clit felt so good, and I couldn't seem to keep the two kinds of masturbating motion going with my left and right hand independently, I was making big odd circles with his cock, so instead I took the showerhead from him and I said, 'You're on your own,' and I sprayed his cock and some of his Danger Mouse T-shirt, that is, *my* Danger Mouse T-shirt, while he began stroking away, staring at my legs and my pussy, and I liked spraying him quite a lot, I liked aiming the water at his fist, I liked the sight of his wet T-shirt, and he had, this is rather bad of me to say, but he had a kind of gruesome-looking cock, a real monster, and the relief of not having that girth in me was itself almost enough to put me over the top, and it looked quite a bit more distinguished through the glint of the spray. But I also wanted the water on me—I wanted to spray him, but I wanted the water flowing on me as well—and suddenly it seemed like the most natural thing in the world, I remembered the elephant woman lifting her knee, and so I reached forward and pulled his hips toward me so that his legs straddled my left leg, and I lifted my knee, and he clamped his thighs around it, and

I let my other leg sprawl so that I was absolutely wide open, and now, when I sprayed his cock and his hand the water streamed down his thighs and then down my thigh and on me. And it was exactly what I wanted, and it started to feel so good, and I said so, and suddenly he started stroking himself incredibly fast, it was this blur, like a *sewing* machine, and he produced this major jet of sperm at a diagonal right into the circular spray of the water, so that it fought against all the drops and was sort of torn apart by them, and he was clamping my leg, my smooth leg, extremely tight with those perfectly water-groomed thighs, and I shifted adroitly so that the poached sperm and hot-water runoff wouldn't pour directly into me and possibly cause trouble, but so that it still poured over me. And then he took the showerhead again, and still holding his cock and still clamping my knee very tight, he sprayed slowly across my hand and my thighs very close with the water until I closed my eyes and came, imagining I was in front of a circus audience. So that was nice."

"God of mercy, I am so jealous!"

"Don't be," she said. "I think my offhand talk of yeast unnerved him, and his subservient streak unnerved *me*. Anyway, the point is, that story is connected to this very call between you and me, because when I was in the shower yesterday, and close to coming—"

"Thinking about the three painters."

"No, *after* the three painters, when I was very close to

149

coming, I was thinking of that time with Lawrence, as I occasionally do, I imagine him handing me my bottles of shampoo with a serious expression, or some fragment of it, anyway yesterday I thought of the Bionic Mike Transmitter that he'd described, and I started to make these very theatrical moans, like 'oh yeah, oh yeah baby, ooh yeah, pump it deep, pump it deep, oooh yeah' and I imagined that someone had left a Bionic Mike Transmitter in my bathroom and that random men on the expressway were driving by with their radios scanning the stations and suddenly they would pick me up, they'd hear me moaning exaggeratedly in the shower. I started to feel myself beginning to come, and I filled my mouth with water, and I thought of the men on the expressway hearing my mouth fill with water, and as I started to come I pushed the water from my mouth so that it poured from my chin over me, which is what I usually do, and I said, and this was not theatrical, this was heartfelt, I said, '*Oh, shoot it, shoot it, you cocksuckers!*' I guess that in my ecstasy I was a trifle confused."

"Perfectly understandable. So then you called tonight . . ."

"I called tonight I think out of the same impulse, the idea that five or six men would hear me come, as if my voice was this *thing*, this disembodied body, out there, and as they moaned they would be overlaying their moans onto it, and, in a way, coming onto it, and the idea appealed to me, but then, when I actually made the call, the reality of it was that the men were so irritating, either passive, wanting me to entertain them, or full of what-are-your-measurements questions, and so I was silent for a while, and then I heard your voice and liked it."

"Thank you. Yours is nice, too, you know. Very smooth."

"Thanks. I just had it waxed yesterday. Shall we, do you think, should we perhaps come soon?"

"Yes. You're absolutely right. Are you naked?"

"Wait a sec. Yes, I am now officially naked, except for the bra."

"Are your legs apart?"

"My toes are holding on to the edge of the coffee table."

"Is your right hand touching your clitoris?"

"How impertinent! But yes, the answer is yes. My clitoris is in fact squeezed between my two index fingers, left and right, which are on either side of it."

"All right. You do whatever you want with those index fingers, and I'll tell you about a kind of sensing device that I own. What it does, it doesn't eavesdrop, it doesn't pick up sounds, it simply senses the presence nearby of any intelligent strumming woman. It looks like an antique pocket watch, it's gold, with a cover, but when you open it, instead of the dial, there is this mysterious fluid, this very special fluid in there that glows in several colors when the right conditions are met, for reasons

151

that are not clear, except that of course a woman masturbating is so important an event in the physical universe that elemental relations in matter are affected as it occurs, and there are these sort of currents in the fluid that slowly move in a certain direction, like lines of force, which give you some sense of where the masturbation signals are coming from, although it takes years of practice, and of course a great deal of native skill as well, to learn how to read the fluid correctly. It's called the Bionic Mmmm-Detector, as you might suspect. Well, I'm driving down the expressway of an eastern city one evening around ten o'clock, in town on business, in my rented midsize car, my Ford Topaz, with the radio going, a classics oldie station, playing 'Ain't Nobody,' and I'm just driving along, and as usual I have my Mmmm-Detector open on the seat beside me, but the fluid is dark, and then I start curving through this residential area, very close to the buildings on either side, and I glance down at the seat beside me, and my God, I'm getting a very strong signal, I'm getting wave patterns I've never seen before, from very near and to my right, and craning my neck I catch sight of a lighted window, and I know that behind it you are in process, you are beginning. My years of practice in reading the flux patterns in the watch tells me this is something very special, something I cannot pass by, and so I palm the steering wheel around suddenly and veer onto the off ramp and scoot back through the narrow streets, swearing at all the one-way signs, and when I come to the door where the

Mmmm-forces are flowing from, I park in a place that is sure to get me a ticket, and I leave my flashers on, and I go into the foyer. There's a row of buttons with names beside them: I hold the detector to each one until one, the third one down, makes the Mmmm-Detector glow with strange colors, and I hesitate, I know that I am interrupting you, and I don't want to do that, that's the last thing I want to do, but it seems so clear to me, reading the force waves, that there is a strong possibility that you would want me to interrupt you, if you knew me, and the conviction that this is true grows in me, and my finger trembles at your button, and there is a huge interior war between reticence and attraction, between the fear that I will inspire fear and the certainty that I should not inspire fear and that we would like each other if I could simply push that button, and I look down at the Mmmm-Detector and I see that you are going to come in less than four minutes if you keep on at that rate, you're really moving, the colors are increasingly intense, and I'm trembling, I'm shivering, but I'm compelled, and I push the button, *bzzzzt.* You're on your bed, and you're wearing a blue long-sleeved pullover sort of shirt, and black pants and black sneakers, but your black pants are around your ankles, and you've got that tattered, disintegrating issue of *Forum* in your left hand, and you're reading about a job interview in which the woman interviewer is sucking the interviewee's cock, and you're right in the middle of things, when *bzzzzt*, the doorbell. Who could that be?"

153

"So I do up my pants and I go to the speaker and I say, 'Hello?' "

"And I say, 'Hi, this is Jim. I know it's late, but I wonder if I could use your phone. My car's engine has seized up, and all the oil lights on the dash are glowing, and I don't dare drive it any further, and the pay phone down the street isn't working.' "

"I say, 'Why did you buzz my apartment?' "

"And I say, 'The others don't answer. You're right to be hesitant, but this isn't a normal situation, this is urgent, I've got to get back to my hotel, I've got a whole day of appointments tomorrow, I just *have* to get seven and a half hours of sleep or I won't function, and I need to use your phone, and I assure you that I'm reasonably sane and peaceable, and I would not normally do this, invade your privacy, but I'm telling you nothing could be more important than this. *Please.*' And you hear the conviction in my voice, and you buzz me in."

"Well, no, first I hold the talk button in and to my empty apartment I call out, 'Jeff? *Jeff!* Enough with the weights! Do you and Mojo Cartilage-Popper mind if someone comes up to use the phone for a second?' *Then* I buzz you in downstairs, knowing that I can look at you through the peephole in my door, and call Bobby the super if you look strange."

"Exactly. I run up to the second floor, and I find your door, and before I stand right in front of it, I check the Mmmm-Sensor and find that your arousal has suffered

154

some decline, you are now ten or more minutes away from an orgasm, though the glow faintly persists. I knock, and I begin pacing back and forth in front of the door, distractedly, like a guy impatient to make a phone call. You look through the peephole and you see this guy, middle height, black hair, not bad-looking, somewhat frazzled, pacing back and forth in front of your door, checking a pocket watch. You let me in. And I introduce myself, I apologize for bothering you, I smile at you, and immediately I can sense the alertness and intelligence in your face, and I see that we understand each other, and I know my Mmmm-Sensor hasn't misled me. Ah, but I've lied my way into your apartment, which is a problem."

"It is, because if I knew!"

"Curtains. So you bring me the phone, and I sit on the edge of a dining-room chair, and I call my answering machine, and I start telling it about the oil lights on my dashboard, I really have to have someone take care of it, I need the number of a cab company, etcetera, and then all of a sudden I stop, in midsentence, and I click off the phone and I say, 'Nah, I can't.' "

" 'You can't what?' "

" 'I can't do it. I can't pretend.' And I confess to you that I've lied, that my car is fine, that I was driving on the expressway, and I got this highly unusual, if not unique, reading on my Mmmm-Sensor, or Mmmm-Detector, whatever I'm calling it, and I pull it out of my pocket and open the finely scratched gold top and show it to you, and I explain, hesitantly, that it, um, picks up the flux currents from intelligent, um, masturbating women, and I show you how it glows, and I point out the wavy flow lines as they move in your direction, and I say, 'They're somewhat fainter now, but they're definitely still there, and they really look great. Now, let's see what happens if I do this.' And I stand next to you, so you can see the Mmmm-Detector as I hold it a foot or so from your face, and then I lower it and slowly pass it a few inches in front of each breast, and the pattern makes these complicated shifts. And I say, 'But as you may be able to see, I'm getting other readings, interference fringes,' and I hold the thing up and I walk slowly to the walls of your hall, where there is a faint rural pattern showing through the paint, and I say, 'For instance, the walls, very curious,' and I shake my head in perplexity, and then I follow the flow lines to a drawer in the kitchen, filled with silverware—very odd—and I follow it into the bathroom, and you follow me in, and I lean into the shower and move the Mmmm-Detector past the fixtures, the drain, the shampoo bottles—beautiful color changes and convergences of flow waves—and I shake my head and I say, 'Gosh, I've never seen anything as rich as this,' and I follow its lead into the bedroom, and you follow me, and I say, 'Wow, *very* high flux levels in here,' and I pass it over your chenille bedspread and I say, 'Your feet must have been here and here,' pointing to two places quite far apart on the bed, and I know that everything I'm doing is forward, is really inexcusable, but in a way you're curious, and I'm just relaying facts, and I sense your willingness to have this happen, and I push the Mmmm-Detector into the pillow and then reach under it and find your disintegrating copy of *Forum*, and I sit down on the bed and page through it slowly, holding the device to each page, until I reach a certain page, and I peer very closely at the sensor, and then I hold it close to the button on your pants, and I inspect it again, and I look up smiling, and I hold the magazine out to you, pointing at something on the page, and I say, 'You were reading this sentence, this phrase right here in this sentence, when I buzzed your apartment.' "

"And," she said, "I take the *Forum* and read what you're pointing at, and you're pretty close, it's not exactly the right phrase, but you've found the right paragraph, anyway. And I don't know quite what to do. I probably should be calling the cops, because you seem to know all this stuff about me, but on the other hand, there you are, and I am still feeling all puffy down below, and you have a certain amount of charm, and an intriguing pocket watch, and so I offer you a, a what? A dry Vermouth on the rocks. And you accept."

"I do, you're right," he said, "and now I'm sitting on an armchair when you come toward me with the drinks, a low sort of armchair, and I have my legs sprawled open in a fairly innocent way, and I just dust off the area of the armchair that's between my legs, indicating that if you want to, you could sit there with no problem and lean back against me, and you do turn and sit there, but you don't lean back, you're leaning forward, and so I have this warm back, covered in loose blue shirt material, in front of me, this miracle of a back, and I take a sip of the drink, and put it down on the table, on a napkin, so it won't leave a ring, and I reach up and click off the table lamp so it's a bit darker, and I close my eyes and find your shoulders with my hands and you ask where I found the Mmmm-Detector and I describe the table of junk I found it on in a flea market in Anaheim, a hundred and forty bucks, without any manual, and how I taught myself over several years what it was for and how to read it, and as I'm telling you this I'm moving my thumbs in two little arcs back and forth above your shoulder blades, which is as much of a back rub as I can handle, because the notion of something called a *back rub* tires my mind out instantly, and I can't do anything that has to do with that, even though your back and my hands are interested in each other. What interests me is your bra, quite honestly, and so I relax my left hand and let it slide down the middle of your back, just let the fingers slide very lightly down over the material of your shirt, until I come to the place where your bra is fastened, and with my eyes closed, and with your ass warm between my legs, but still innocently there, I feel the three possible places for the hooks on the little fastener to hook, and that you've used the third setting, because of shrinkage probably, and I take my fingers and I follow the upward curving edge of the bra as it rises toward your shoulders, and I ride this curve up a little way over your shoulders and then back down your back and in to the middle again. It's like driving over the Bay Bridge. Then I follow the bottom edge horizontally around, under your arms, until I just reach the seam where a cup begins, and you feel all this somewhat dimly, because it's through your shirt and through the bra, but you are more aware now of the shape of the bra that you're wearing, and then I go back to the fastener and I make that time-honored pinching move and release the hooks through your shirt, and each side pulls away, and now I feel that I have this perfect central stretch with no interruption, and I press my left palm between your shoulder blades and slide slowly down, moving your shirt, feeling wrinkles in it form and pass, and I can feel some slight bumps of your backbone—what a beautiful back, so warm. I want very much to feel your skin. So I put both hands on your hips and hook my two thumbs and index fingers under the bottom edge of your shirt, or no, I grab hold of it on either side and pull it, because it was tucked into your pants, and I pull it out, and then I hook my hands underneath, and I can feel your skin move slightly as my fingers first touch it, just above your hips, and I run my fingers back along the inside of your waistband, and I can feel the warmth of your ass, and then I flatten my hands against your back and slide them up under your shirt, ah, all the way up so the fingers come out and go a little way along the nape of your neck into your hair before subsiding. It's a loose shirt, don't worry. Am I going too slow for you?"

"No no, keep going, that's fine."

"Oh, I love moving my hands over you under your loose shirt, I love that. I'd slide my hands around over your stomach, so that my fingertips met, and feel it pull in, and slide up slowly along your ribs, and when I got to where the curves of your breasts started, I would trace them around, out to the sides, back to the middle, and I would pass just my fingertips up between your breasts, up along your breastbone, pushing under the loose bra, and then one finger even higher, along your voice box, to where your chin starts, and you'd lean your head back and I would be able to smell your hair, and then I'd pull back down, deliberately avoiding your breasts."

"And I would stand up," she said, "and turn around so I'm facing you, with my shins touching the armchair, and I'd undo the button of my pants."

"And I would reach out," he said, "and take hold of your zipper and push it slowly down, so that I'm pushing against your mound with it, not at your clitoris, but above it, and I'd slide my fingers under your waistband and guide your pants off over your hips and ass, and when they fell to your knees I'd put my foot on the inside of the crotch so you could step out of them easily, and I'd smell how wet you are, and I'd slide my hands up your legs and slip my fingers under the waistband of your underpants, and pull them down a little, and then I'd roll them under my palms, so the fabric just rolled up, and they fell and you stepped easily out of them, too. And then . . ."

"And then," she said, "you'd undo your belt and the top button of your pants, and the clink of your belt buckle would be like the little bell signaling the start of something serious, and I would slowly move the zipper over the high lump of your erection, and you'd lift your hips and I'd pull your pants off, but not your underpants, and then I'd slide one knee on the cushion of the armchair, between your legs, against your balls, and the other outside your legs, and I'd let my weight settle on your thigh, so we're close but facing each other."

"And first," he said, "my leg would feel the roughness of your pubic hair, I'd feel it scratching against itself, and then I'd feel you open and I'd feel this wet oval of heat on the muscle of my thigh, and I'd look down at your folded legs straddling my leg, and run my hands up them, and scoop up your shirt again, and this time I'd lift it with me as my hands moved up, and I'd watch them, I watch your shirt rising, the seam of your shirt is over my wrists, and then I reach your breasts and I lift your shirt and your loose bra up just a little more, and, ah, there they are your nipples, finally, and you see my hands reveal them, and I see your breasts moving slightly as you breathe, and

I sit up and bend toward them, and then on second thought straighten and lick my lips and kiss you, and your tongue is very warm and very friendly."

"Whoo!"

"And I bend back down toward one of your breasts, and I open my mouth, which now finally remembers how to kiss from just kissing you, and I just breathe on your nipple, and the shirt starts to fall down over it, and I nudge it aside with my tongue and then hold it out of the way with my hand, and now I have your breast entirely surrounded with both my palms, and you feel your breast held this way, completely under my care, and I just touch the tip of my tongue once to the almost flat top of your nipple, which is hard, and then I open my mouth quite wide, and draw my tongue way back, and you arch your back slightly, and so my lips make contact with your breast, surrounding your nipple but *not* touching it, and I suck on it without touching it also, so that you feel the pulling as it's being drawn into my mouth, and even becoming soft, or losing its definition, from being drawn in that way, and wanting to be directly touched, and then you feel the tip of my tongue just touch the base of your nipple and then paint a warm vertical stripe up over it, and then back down, and then my whole tongue, much wider and fatter, pushes and moves against your nipple, and then I hold my mouth and tongue still and a little looser and with my hands I move your whole breast in circles and back and forth under them, so that you feel its

whole size in my hands, ho, I'm sucking on your
breasts . . ."

"And I'd hold on to your head as you sucked my
breasts, and feel your tongue doing all those nice things
to me through your cheeks. I am so *wet*."

"Oh, and I'd tighten my thigh muscle where your
pussy was pressing down on it and feel your wetness slide
against me, and I'd look up at you and kiss you again,
and slide my hands down to your hips and push down, so
that there was more pressure still against your notch, and
I'd feel your hips move slightly, adjusting themselves so
that it felt best . . ."

"And while we were kissing I'd reach down and catch
my fingers under one leg hole of your underpants and
pull it up and over your cock and balls and then I'd hold
your balls in my hand for a second and then I'd bring my
hand up and squeeze the head of your cock in my fist and
kind of pull and push on it while I was squeezing it
tightly."

"And you'd feel my lips making an *oh* shape while we
were kissing, with the pleasure of your hand doing that,
and, ho, I'd need to suck your clit soon, because I'd feel
the come in me starting to want to spurt out, and so we'd
shift positions so that you were sitting on the armchair
and I was kneeling on the floor, and you'd scoot your
hips forward so that your ass was just at the edge of the
pillow, and when you glanced down you could see your
own breasts, and your pubic hair, and your knees held

together, with my hands on them, and you'd see the glossy wet place on my thigh, and then I'd encircle your legs with one arm, holding them together, and bend toward your bush and breathe on it, the little of it I can see, and I run my fingers just down the long place where the insides of your thighs touch, all the way to your knees, and then I'd let go of your legs, and they'd fall slightly apart, and as my hands started to move up inside them, with my fingers splayed wide, they'd move farther and farther apart, and then I'd lift your knees and hook them over the arms of the armchair, so that you were wide open for me, and in the darkness your bush would still be indistinct, and I'd look up at you, and I'd move on my knees so I'm closer, so I could slide my cock in you if I wanted, and I touch your shoulders with my hands, and pass my fingertips all the way down over your breasts and over your stomach and just lightly over your bush, just to feel the hair, and then I say, 'I'm going to lick you now,' and I lick both your nipples once very briefly good-bye, and I breathe my way down, and I pass over your bush this time with my mouth, and I see where the tan stops, and where the hair begins, and I keep going, and your legs are spread wide, and so I kiss inside one knee, and then across to the other, and up, back and forth, and at the end of each kiss I give a little upward lick with my tongue, up lick, lick, lick, back and forth, moving closer and closer to where your thighs meet. And then the last time I turn my head, there's nothing I can do, my mouth is just buried in your pubic hair, and I breathe through it, I fill it with warmth, and I open my mouth more, and I bring my tongue out, and I start low, and the underside of my tongue is touching my lower teeth, and I lick slowly upwards, until I reach the place where the skin is more folded, and I find that beautiful clitoris, and I move over it with my tongue, and then when I've found it I close my mouth and sort of burrow my way into you so that all your pubic hair is away from my mouth, and my mouth is entirely around your clit, and I hold my hands very high on the insides of your thighs, feeling those stretched tendons, so you feel how wide apart you are, and I suck the skin around your clitoris into my mouth, like I did with your nipple, so that you feel it drawn into my mouth, and when you feel it drawn in I take my tongue, very high, right at the base of your clitoris, where I can feel that little ridge beginning, and I start to go back and forth over it, back and forth slowly over it, and you feel the tip of my tongue traveling down toward the part where it's hotter, and then I reach the very full part of your clitoris, and you pull your hips in slightly and re-adjust to that feeling, and I cup my hands under your ass and lift you into my mouth and just *suck* on you, and I shake my whole head back and forth very fast, as if I'm saying, no, no, no, but I'm saying yes to your clit with my tongue."

"Oh, I'm going to come soon. Put your cock in me, I want to think about your cock in me."

"Are your legs spread apart?"

"Yes."

"Oh, and you're stroking that clit?"

"Yes."

"Okay, so I'd take one last long up-lick on your pussy and then I'd straighten up, and I'd still be cupping your ass in my hands, and you'd be completely visible by now, wide open, sopping wet, and I'd take my cock in one hand and kind of vibrate it over your clit, and you'd slide your hands down and hold your lips apart with your fingers, and then I'd push my cock down and I'd feel how hot you were and I'd have to slide myself slowly all the way in, and then I'd pull almost all the way out again and slide in, into that nice nasturtium, and each time I pulled out I'd be able to see your hand circling your clit, and I'd slide in until my pubic bone thumped against you, and I'd watch your breasts move each time I reached this limit, and we would be fucking, sliding in and out . . ."

"Oh!"

"And your finger would be flying over your clit, your hand would be lifted and your finger would be flying back and forth, and I'd have your asscheeks cupped in both my hands, so you could feel a pulling on your asshole, and I would be sliding with long strokes out, and in, and out, and in, and I'd see your tits moving each time . . ."

"Oh! *Oh!*"

"Oh, I'm starting to come for you, my cock is pumping inside you . . ."

"*Oh!* Nnnnnnnn! Nnn! Nnn! Nnn! Nnn! Nnn! Nnn!"

"It's spurting out! I can't help it! Ah! Ah! Oooooo."

There was a pause.

"Oh man," she said. "Wow. You there?"

"I think so." He swallowed. "Let me catch my breath."

"That was—that was—*man*," she said. "I saw the great seal of the Commonwealth of Massachusetts when I came."

"I heard you come and I came," he said.

"Whoo! How long have we been talking?"

"Hours and hours."

"Hours and hours and hours," she said. "My mouth is chapped. Too much making out."

"Is your voice sore?"

"It really is. Whoo! Gee, I'm going to have to call in sick *again*. I'll sleep all day, mm, sounds delightful. The hiss on the phone is very loud now, isn't it? That companionable hiss. It's always louder at the end of conversations."

"Oh, is it the end already?" he said. "Couldn't we just fade out somehow, talking and talking? I can't think of a better way to invest my life savings. Not that I'm much of a saver."

"You're quite a telephoner, though."

"You are too! I mean it! I think really this is one of the nicest conversations I've ever had."

"I liked it too," she said. "I don't know, though—do you think we talked enough about sex?"

"Not nearly enough. I—"

"Yes?" she said.

"Do you think our . . . wires will cross again?"

"I don't know. I don't know. What do you think?"

"I could give you my number," he said. "I mean if you still want it. I'll avoid a possibly awkward moment by not asking for yours. Or we could meet out here again, if you'd rather do that."

"Out here under the stars? I can't afford it. Where's a pencil? Ah, a nice blunt pencil. Tell me your number."

He told her. She read it back to him.

"Call me soon," he said. "In fact, call me in a few hours, after you've topped yourself off in the shower."

"You know me too well."

"I like you a lot."

"I wonder what you look like," she said.

"Surprisingly normal. Maybe someday you'll know."

"It's a possibility."

"We'd probably be a little nervous at first, if we met. But then . . ."

"Then we'd start masturbating like ferrets," she said, "and that would quickly break the ice."

"That's right. I hope you will call. You remember I have this pair of cotton pointelle tights. Unopened."

"Size small?"

"Size small. In faun. Put Leona to work, get those legs waxed, I'm on my way. No. But call me soon. Soon soon soon. I hope you will."

"All right," she said. "Let me think about things. Let me absorb the strangeness."

"What's strange?"

"Nothing," she said. "I guess nothing. I think I should probably sign off now, though. I have to put a load of towels in the laundry."

"Certainly. Okay. Thank you for calling this number."

"Thank *you*. Bye Jim."

"Bye Abby. Bye."

They hung up.

For further information about Granta Books
and a full list of titles, please write to us at

Granta Books

2/3 HANOVER YARD

NOEL ROAD

LONDON

N1 8BE

enclosing a stamped, addressed envelope

———————————

You can visit our website at

http://www.granta.com